Praise for Rites: Stories

"Savannah Johnston in her debut collection *Rites: Stories* is shown to be a writer of beautifully and calmly compressed prose and sly, powerful storytelling. This is an honest writer at work, the details seem to have been lived among and observed and smelled and smoked. Her characters never have enough money, the truck won't move anymore, the dog food plant isn't hiring, here's a beer. These people, in their poverty and lessening hope, are written with clear-eyed love; Savannah Johnston never looks away or condemns, and that's the high-water mark for me."

 —Daniel Woodrell, author of *Winter's Bone* and *The Maid's Version*

"From the first few lines of Savannah Johnston's *Rites*, we know we're in for a wild, beautiful ride in Indian country. The language sings with a kind of tenderness and toughness that is so rare and so lovely. And her characters? They will break your heart."

 —Erika Wurth, author of *Buckskin Cocaine* and *Crazy Horse's Girlfriend*

"Savannah Johnston offers us characters neglected, marginalized, hurt and hurting others, with brutal honesty and intensity that's nuanced and unsentimental. Her writing deftly peels away the layers that make people who they are, not to ask for forgiveness or pity for her characters, but to make us pay attention to how hard it is to be a person in the world."

 —Dima Alzayat, author of *Alligator and Other Stories*

"In prose that is stark and revealing, poetic and profoundly soulful, Savannah Johnston connects the reader with characters who, ignored or marginalized by larger society, grapple with the obstacles that have come to define their existence with a richness of humility and admirable grit. Reading *Rites,* I felt honored to be a guest in their world, and their stories will stay with me."

    —Linda LeGarde Grover, author of *In the Night of Memory*

"An electric collection—Savannah Johnston's *Rites* depicts the lives of Oklahomans with an unflinching eye, in dazzling prose. These stories are vivid, intimate, and bound to break your heart in the best possible ways."

    —Allegra Hyde, author of *Of This New World*

"In Savannah Johnston's *Rites*, we see a young girl who is just tall enough to leave the kiddie rides for the carnival's true thrills and dangers. In another moment, a young driver sees the road differently after her first lesson behind the wheel. Johnston picks the breakthrough moments that give her writing a compelling sense of motion and energy. She creates the rituals that her characters know well and the private ones they create for themselves. These stories show the contours of home with the mix of familiarity and mystery that give this collection its charge and texture."

    —Ravi Howard, author of *Driving the King*

"These stories are raw postcards from an America that has found its chronicler. Unflinching and honest, Savannah Johnston's compelling work, her necessary Choctaw voice, is an important addition to contemporary fiction."
—Sabina Murray, PEN/Faulkner Award winner, author of *The Human Zoo* and *Valiant Gentlemen*

"From funerals to biker bars, riverbanks to back roads, *Rites* portrays rural, Native Oklahoma as gritty and gentle, violent and welcoming—as a full, complicated place. The heartbreak and heartstrings both are held close through these stories. With prose that snaps and crackles like a lightning strike, Savannah Johnston's debut delivers stories that don't flinch."
—Toni Jensen, author of *Carry* and *From the Hilltop*

"In direct and honest prose, Savannah Johnston writes with great compassion about the difficult lives of her characters in rural Oklahoma. This is a stunning debut."
—Chris Offutt, author of *The Killing Hills*

RITES: STORIES

RITES: STORIES

By Savannah Johnston

Published by Jaded Ibis Press.
www.jadedibispress.com

JADED IBIS PRESS

To my mother.

TABLE OF CONTENTS

Rites

When I was eight, Papa Tushka crashed his Chevy Malibu through the front of McCoy's Texaco. Steve McCoy went to high school with Mama, and he didn't file charges. Papa blew way over the limit on the field test, but he swore it was a setup. He kept a loaded assault rifle next to the front door and a handgun under the seat of his truck.

"Never trust a man in a suit," he said.

As the procession pulled graveside, the valley clouded over. A wall cloud brewed in the east. The funeral home pitched a tent and set up a few dozen plastic chairs, throwing in a bouquet of white lilies for an extra fifty dollars. Papa's grave was beside a plum tree. Our house, a split-level clapboard heap, sat slightly askew on top of Digger's Hill, next to the cemetery. I could see my bike propped against the porch from my folding chair under the tent. The graveside had a pretty big turnout, and I could barely hear the priest over the blowing noses and muffled sobs. The Catholic priest was the only preacher in town who'd do the service for free, and the tribe only covered half the cost of the funeral home. I heard Mama and Uncle Jake talking about it. We buried Papa Tushka in a plastic casket.

We all lived in Papa's house: Papa, Nana, Mama, me, my sister Lucy, Uncle Jake, and Aunt Judy's girls, Angie and Karen. Aunt Judy lived in a trailer in Wynona. Uncle Jake said she was a two-bit junky whore, but we only saw her at Christmas.

Papa was a champion bareback bronc rider despite four broken noses, a dislocated shoulder, two collapsed lungs, and a fractured vertebra. He had a bite-shaped scar on the back of his neck from a bar brawl in Clinton that left the knuckles of his right hand crushed and knobby. Once, Uncle Jake shot him with a pellet gun. Papa laughed and pushed the metal BB out of his cheek. He popped the BB in his mouth and swallowed it.

He died on a Wednesday. Some farmer saw the accident, said the truck was swerving before it ran off the bridge. Clipped a low-hanging branch on the way down and ripped the cab clean through. The paramedics used the Jaws of Life to cut Papa out of the front seat.

Mama told me I was Papa's favorite because I wore my hair in braids like he did. Papa wrapped his braids in strips of red cloth like the singers at the powwow. My braids were skinny and the color of straw.

The night Papa died, Uncle Jake caught me sitting on his bucket in the garage. The house was more crowded than ever with Papa and Nana's friends, and I didn't like to cry where anyone could see me. Uncle Jake sat down on the steel frame of a car he was stripping, a bottle of beer in his hand. He took a sip and lit a smoke. He had a heavy, silver lighter that clicked shut.

"What're you doin' in here, Tree?" His mustache bristled as he chewed the filter.

"I didn't want to stay in there anymore," I said. I tucked my knees into my T-shirt.

"Yeah, I hear ya," Uncle Jake said. "You okay?"

"Yeah," I said. I stared at a pile of cat litter soaking up an oil slick. "Do you think Papa's in hell?"

Uncle Jake chuckled. "That'd be about right, huh?" I let out a little cry, and he straightened up. "Nah, nah, I'm just kidding. Don't let any of that hell shit get under your skin." He sucked on his smoke and exhaled through his nose. He looked out through the open garage door and waved his arm across the sky. "See those stars? I like to think that's the spirit of the Tushkas. Each and every one of us'll be up there someday, lookin' down on what's left."

I sniffled. "That sounds alright."

"Pretty good, huh?" he said. He swigged the rest of his beer. "I got it from *The Lion King*."

Papa was afraid of flying, crowds, and cops. He didn't trust doctors or insurance men, and he slept upside down in a recliner. He said it relieved the pressure.

The funeral reception was a tribal affair at the Community Center, and Francis Strike Axe manned the door. He had a smoldering bundle of sage that he waved over everyone as they came in. It was supposed to get rid of the bad spirits anyone might be carrying around, but I still felt an angry knot in my chest. Mama was busy taking care of Nana, so I stuck close to Uncle Jake. After he made the rounds, grasping my shoulder and nodding gravely at all the well-wishers, he pointed me toward the buffet and headed to the back. Angie was showing Karen and Lucy the crooked hoop earring she pierced her own belly button with. It had bled through the front of her dress. I turned and followed him.

I found him back by the Center's air conditioner smoking a hand-rolled cigarette. The smell was sweet like pine needles. He held the cigarette behind his back.

"Go on inside," he said. "I'll be in in a sec." He coughed.

"I'll wait," I said. I sat on the air conditioner next to him. I pointed at his cigarette. "That smells nice."

"Shit," he said. He dug the heel of his boot in the gravel. "How old are you now?"

"Twelve and a half," I said. I smoothed my black dress over my knees. There was white cat hair stuck in its weave.

Uncle Jake sighed. "It's a joint, girl," he said. "You know, weed?"

"It smells like Nana's room."

"Now you know the Tushka secret," Uncle Jake said. He held up the joint and pointed to the wet crease along the paper's gum. "We're a bunch of stoners."

Inside, the dinner was starting. I heard Greg Murphy, Papa's best VFW buddy, giving orders to try his wife's chili.

I didn't notice when Papa was drunk, like I never noticed when Nana, Uncle Jake, or even Mama had been smoking pot. These were just states they sometimes occupied. Papa was funnier after a few drinks, mostly.

When Lucy was a baby, Papa's yappy little dog snapped at her, and Mama kicked it across the room. He yanked Mama by the back of her dress and threw her out of the house. Papa sat in the doorway with the assault rifle across his lap and lectured the empty driveway on the merits of responsible dog ownership.

"If you wanna act like an animal," he shouted into the dark, "you can sleep with the coyotes, all of you!"

He fell asleep there. Mama woke him up when she came

home in the morning and made him a pot of coffee.

I sat next to Mama on the couch when she called our relatives. She had Papa's rolodex on her lap and was flicking quickly through the cards, running the tip of her finger over each number as she swung the dial on the old rotary phone. Papa filed Aunt Judy under *U*, penciling in *ungrateful*. Mama choked when she saw it, smiled a little, and began to cry again. Her eyeliner ran into the bags beneath her eyes, and her nose was red and swollen. We had the same straight nose.

I didn't know what to say to her.

Mama wiped her eyes and hugged me to her chest. She was wearing a sweater she'd cut the neck out of, and I could see two sets of footprints tattooed on her chest. The set on the left was mine, *Treena* written in script beside it. The other was Lucy's, but Mama hadn't gotten the money together to get her name, too.

"My biggest baby," she said into my hair. "I miss him, Tree."

She kissed the top of my head and rubbed my back. It made my skin itch, but I let her do it. I didn't want to make her take care of me. I bit my lip, grinding my teeth over the inside of my cheek at the same time. I felt a hiccupping sob waiting in my throat, and I swallowed it.

The night before the funeral, Mama and Uncle Jake took Nana to the bar; the VFW was throwing a wake of its own. Mama left Angie in charge. Angie, Karen, Lucy and I were sleeping in the living room, and we watched a handful of Disney movies before Angie wanted to do something else.

"I know a game," she said. "It's called Night Light, and what you do is you put your arms like this"—she crossed her arms over her chest—"and hold your head down"—she leaned forward as if to touch her toes—"and you breathe really fast, then push yourself on the wall"—she reared back against it—

"and then somebody pushes on your chest, and you pass out." She put her hands on her hips. "Who's first?"

Karen stepped forward. She was much darker than Angie, probably because her dad was rumored to be Mexican. That's what Papa said, anyway. I watched Angie directing her from my seat on the floor.

"Are you gonna do it?" Lucy sat next to me on the floor.

"Pfft," I blew a raspberry. "No. It's stupid."

Angie let Karen double over and pant. She narrowed her eyes at me. "You've been weird all week. What's wrong with you?"

"What if Karen goes retarded or something? What if you hurt her?" I asked. Lucy nodded beside me.

"I've done it!" Angie said. She turned to Karen. "Now, up!"

Karen threw herself back on the wall, and Angie pressed hard on her collarbone with both hands. Karen gasped for a second, and then her eyes rolled back, and she slid down. Angie let her fall to the floor, grinning from ear to ear. Lucy pulled on my arm.

"Oh man, oh man," Lucy whispered. Her nails dug into my skin.

Karen came to a few seconds later, cross-eyed and mumbling.

"Did you like it?" she asked. "It's fun, right?"

Karen smiled and nodded. "I wanna do it again!"

"Not yet. It's someone else's turn," Angie said. She fished a potato chip out of a bag on the couch. "Who's next?"

After the army band played and they gave Nana the flag, the pallbearers lowered Papa's casket into the ground. Most of the crowd headed straight for their cars, eager to change clothes and get to the reception. The hearse drove Mama and Nana home, and Uncle Jake agreed to take us home in Nana's Lincoln. He was talking to someone by the road, passing a cigarette between them. The funeral director asked us to give up our seats, so they could pack everything up. We waited under the plum tree.

When he finished, he came and stood next to the grave. "One last service for the old man, huh?" he said. He motioned for us to get up and join hands, and we did. "Everybody close your eyes." I didn't. "You, too, Tree." Uncle Jake took a deep breath. "Papa Tushka, Father, Grandfather—you were kind of an asshole." Lucy squeaked and almost jerked her hand from mine. I squeezed her fingers. "But either way, we'll miss you." I squinted out from one eye. Uncle Jake was looking at the sky. "Amen. Now spit!" He spit on the dirt, and Angie was the only one to follow suit. "And run!" He took off toward Nana's Lincoln, whooping like a kid.

MISSING

It had rained the night before, and the road was wet. Joe downshifted Diane's purple pickup truck and gently gassed it, letting it slowly work its way up the hill. Hippie's camper was at the top of the hill. Joe took a drag on his cigarette and exhaled through his nose. He filled out five job applications that day, none for jobs he actually wanted. His clothes still smelled like the dog food factory, where he'd waited in the HR department for an interview. They told him they'd call.

He unbuttoned his collar, tugging the neck open. He hated dressing up for interviews. The jobs never asked for more than jeans, steel-toed boots, and an undershirt. For two weeks, Hippie had been silent about the gig he'd promised, and Diane was starting to get worried. As it was, her mother kept the baby during the day, but if Joe didn't get a job quick, Diane intended to stick him with the baby while she ran the register at EZ Shop. The baby was six months old, and Joe hadn't yet learned how to change a diaper. It rarely registered that the wrinkly, tiny old-man face belonged to his daughter.

A red Jeep was parked in front of the camper, next to Hippie's Cadillac. Joe parked behind the Cadillac, letting the truck's engine idle down before he got out. The Jeep had Texas plates, and a rosary dangled from the rearview mirror. Joe went to the spigot outside the camper and pumped the handle. The water that came out was red with rust, but it flowed clean after a minute or two. He ran his hands under the cool water and splashed his face. It was hot, nearing a hundred degrees. Joe noticed that the utility lines from the camper were unplugged and the generator looked like it had blown out.

The camper door banged behind him, and he swiveled on his heels. Hippie jumped over the camper's steps and jogged to him. Hippie was thinner, and large, purple circles ringed his red eyes. A purple-green bruise flowered on his cheek.

"Hey, Hip," Joe said. "Scared me there."

"What—" Hippie twittered. His hands were shaking. "What are you doing here?"

"I called, man," Joe said. "Hadn't heard from you in a few days."

"You gotta leave, Joe," Hippie said. He didn't make eye contact; he looked at the uprooted stump of a dead redbud. "You gotta get back in the car and go."

"What are you talking about?" Joe asked. He backed up toward the car.

"Just *go*," Hippie said. He kicked at the grass, and Joe saw he had no shoes on. "What're you standing there for? Get the fuck outta here!"

Joe held his hands up. "Alright, alright." He walked back to the Datsun. "You okay in there, man?" He motioned to the Jeep.

"Get outta here!" Hippie shouted. His voice cracked. "Go."

Joe spit to the side. He got in and started the car, backing out before driving away. In the rearview mirror, Hippie turned and went back into the camper. The camper shook as the door slammed shut.

Hippie and Joe lay on the hood of the rust-colored Cadillac. Earlier in the afternoon, a case of Coors on the backseat, they parked outside the airfield's chain-link fence. The air was warm and thick. Joe leaned against the windshield, the glass cool on his back. For a long time, neither man spoke, both nursing beers and Camel cigarettes.

In the distance, a fighter plane's engine whirred to life and began to make its way down the tarmac. The turbines hummed, and the plane taxied around the bend, picking up speed as it rolled toward the Cadillac. Joe elbowed Hippie in the ribs.

"Look alive," he said. He tossed his beer can into the grass. "This is a new one, I'd say. I don't recognize the paint job . . ."

"Mm-hm," Hippie murmured.

Hippie looked disinterestedly across the field. He drew his head up and rubbed his eyes with his fists. His cigarette had burnt out, and he dropped the charred filter. Just short of the fence, the fighter plane lifted off the ground and shot over them. He caught his breath and gave a low whistle.

"Wild, Joe, real wild," he said. He punched him lightly in the bicep. "Let's get outta here. Let's go to Lyle's or someplace."

Joe stared ahead at the hangar across the field. "I'd say that was a A-10, A-10 something, I forget the last part." Joe fished a smashed cigarette from his pocket, straightened it out, and lit the end. "You know how much they pay you to fly them suckers?"

"Not enough, man," he said.

Hippie swung his legs off the hood and grabbed a beer from the last case in the back. The sun was beginning to set, and fireflies were starting to flicker beneath the trees. He cracked the beer's tab.

"I watch movies, dude." Hippie took a long drink. *"Full Metal Jacket, Coming Home*—military's bad for your health."

"That's not the Air Force," Joe said.

Hippie pinched one nostril, blowing hard; a string of snot slapped into the grass. He thought for a minute. "What about *Top Gun*? You don't want to get Goosed."

Joe laughed. "Grab me a beer?"

Hippie hopped off the hood and scooped one from the case. The cans were warm. He handed it over.

"Yep," Joe said. "Good money. Did you try for that rig over in Chickasha?"

"Nah, I'm working on something a little higher-end," Hippie said. He reclined on the hood and crossed his boots. "Diane's still got that gig at EZ Shop, right?"

"Yeah, but babies are fucking expensive, dude. I need a job," Joe said. He drank his beer in long gulps.

"No reason you can't go in forty-sixty," Hippie said. "I'm still working out the details, but it's gonna be big."

"How come not fifty-fifty?" Joe asked.

"They're private people, these guys. I'm gonna have to work the personal end," he said. Another fighter plane rattled toward them. "Give me a week or two to get it all straightened out."

"What kind of gig is it?" Joe asked. "Am I looking at two to five, or ten to twenty?"

"You're looking at gold, man," Hippie said. The plane rumbled overhead; Joe tried to say something, but the engine drowned him out.

Carl rapped his knuckles on the washed oak door. His hair was greasy and slicked back against his head. He wore the flannel button-up just as he had every day for three years. The DOC had thought to give him new jeans, though. Since his release two weeks before, he'd kept a room in Del City with a hooker named Angel. She wasn't happy when he tried to pay her in vouchers.

A Greyhound dropped him at the post office, and he walked from there. After three miles, he knocked on Mama Carson's door. She lived next to the old school in a stone house built into the hill. Carl hadn't told her he was coming.

The door clicked open, and Mama Carson stuck her head out. "Yes?"

"Hi, Ma," he said. He smiled, and he could tell by her expression she'd forgotten about his front teeth. "How's it going?"

"Oh, Carl," Mama Carson said. She sighed and held up a half-empty bottle of gin. "Well, if you're here, you might as well come in."

She opened the door and waved him in. The lights were off in the living room, but she had the television turned on, the volume low. *Family Ties* was on. Mama Carson walked as if her feet hurt, and she sat heavily in a dusty armchair.

"So," she began, "what's the news?"

Carl sat opposite her on the couch. Her chair was directly in front of the television, and she immediately appeared to be watching. The kitchenette opened into the living room, and he noticed that she had taken off all the cabinet doors. Inside, the cabinets were bare. A cat curled up in the bread basket.

"I'm . . . well, I'm out," Carl started. He rubbed his knuckles. "And I'm looking for a job. I need a place to stay for a while, you know." He glanced around the room: He guessed most everything had been pawned. Bail is higher for repeat offenders. Mama Carson's hands shook as she brought the bottle to her lips. "Seen Robbie around? Maybe he could get me on at his rig. I could stay with him, if it's too much trouble—"

"Ha!" Mama Carson interrupted. For a second, Carl thought she was laughing at the television, but she suddenly turned to him. "No one calls him Robbie these days, Carl.

I haven't seen Robbie." She shook her head. "Haven't seen Hippie. You can ask him if you find him."

Carl looked at his mother's feet. They were swollen and sockless, splotchy with busted veins. Her house had a sour smell. She lolled her head back toward the television.

"You can stay if you want." She passed her hand through the air. "Plenty of space."

Carl stood and went to the refrigerator. He opened it, hoping to find something to drink, only to see thirteen cans of cat food, two liters of gin, and two limes.

Gena tightened a belt around her arm. She whimpered and looked at Hippie expectantly. In the dark of his camper, he rolled away from her and laughed. When he got up, the pop-out bed rose a little before settling under Gena's weight. He rubbed the soles of his feet across the plastic floor, tugging on a pair of underwear. Gena pulled the blankets up to her armpits and frowned.

"You're hogging it," she said.

She picked through the ashtray on the windowsill for half-smoked cigarettes. They were all smoked down to the filter. She groaned and reached for her purse, pulling a cigarette out of a nearly full pack.

"You've just got rich in your blood, don't ya, honey?" Hippie smiled at her as he put a pot of coffee on the stove.

The past couple of days, he'd gone a little out of his mind, but after sleeping for seventeen hours, he felt better. His jaw was tight from grinding his teeth, and he felt as if his marrow had been scraped out. He imagined Gena sucking the marrow out of his bones. It made his teeth hurt.

"Baby, you said you had lots," she whined.

"Baby, I do," he said. He snatched her cigarette and took a long drag on it. "But that's business. Pleasure is different. And you already shot up more than half my cut."

She let the sheet fall. She got the impression Hippie was intimidated by her breasts.

"If that's your half, it must not be so big-time after all," she said. Hippie turned to her slowly. His eyes went to her breasts, then to her face. She flipped her hair over her shoulder. "What? Not what you wanted to hear?"

He waved his hand at her and turned down the coffee. He got a cigarette from his pack on the table and lit it. The camper wasn't more than a kitchen with a back panel that came down into a large twin bed. When the bed was down, it blocked the oven, but Hippie liked that he could start coffee from bed. He leaned against the countertop and played with the lever on the toaster.

"I was hoping you'd be a little nicer, you know, after I just gave you a free ride for three days," Hippie said. The crank had him strung out, and he wanted a joint.

"Hippie, baby, come on," Gena said. She lay on her stomach and reached out to him. He was jealous that she looked fine, acted as if she felt fine, when he felt so off. "What's it gonna hurt? There's lots more where that came from—you said so yourself."

Hippie crossed his arms and thought about it for a split second before he popped open the cabinet and plucked a saran-wrapped rock from a bigger bag of the same.

"Okay, but no shooting this one," he said. He began to break it up on the table. "It lasts longer if you toot it."

Joe and Hippie were drunk on Schnapps, driving the Cadillac in long, lazy loops around the A-frame house Joe rented from his mother-in-law. Hippie was in the driver's seat, wrenching the cork steering wheel he'd ordered special as if it could save his life. Joe couldn't help but admire the mechanics of General Motors' hydraulic power steering. The four-door sedan made each turn smoothly, gliding silently across the grass, narrowly avoiding the fence he was in the process of putting up between the backyard and the lot behind it.

It was well past midnight; Diane was asleep or pretending to be, and the baby was fine. Joe admitted he didn't know whether or not the baby was fine, but he figured Diane would clue him in if something came up. This was his approach to most things.

Hippie slammed on the brakes, and Joe was thankful for the antilock braking system. Joe propped his head up in the open window and saw the dark circles they'd drawn around the house. Hippie patted his shoulder.

"Your turn!"

The two men traded places, Hippie crawling out the driver's side and beating his palms over the hood as he climbed into the passenger seat. Joe pulled himself across the bench seat, scooting forward to reach the pedals. He couldn't muster Hippie's enthusiasm, and the headlights swam before his eyes. He put the car in drive and pressed the gas, a little too hard. The Cadillac jolted forward, and Joe let up quickly.

"Ease into it," Hippie said. "You're gonna be my driver once I get this shit up off the ground. I need you to handle Cordelia with expert hands."

"Cordelia?" Joe slurred.

"The car," Hippie said quickly. "My car. I call her Cordelia."

Joe gently accelerated and swung the car in a tight loop around a scrubby oak. Straightening out, he closed one bleary eye and tried to steer the car into the old tracks.

"When'd you decide to call her that?" Joe asked. He was drunker than he'd thought.

"Just now! You don't like it?" Hippie waved both hands out in front of him, jittery. He smelled like crank, and his skin was yellow.

Joe ignored the smell and kept his eyes on the road. "Nah, it's fine, it's fine." He thought for a second. "What about Delilah? That's a good name. That's a Bible name."

"She handles like a Cordelia," Hippie said. "Hey, check this out."

Hippie reached into his waistband and produced a small revolver. Hippie held it gently with both hands, his right hand loosely gripping the butt of the gun. Joe stared straight ahead.

"I'm drivin', Hip," he said.

"You're already in the yard so come on, look," Hippie said. He held the gun higher, dangling it in Joe's face. Joe squinted past it to the grass illuminated by the headlights.

"Where'd you come by it?" Joe asked. Hippie had his head out the window. "D'you do the job without me?" Hippie sat back against the seat but didn't look at him. "Dammit, you did, didn't you? Man, I've been waiting for this job!"

Hippie snapped forward and fired a shot into the air. The wide night caught the sound and ricocheted it back. Joe jumped and let his foot off the accelerator. The car slowed and gently ran up against a sapling, bending the little tree under the front fender. Hippie turned and looked at Joe, his eyes bright with excitement. He crowed.

"Whew!" Hippie laughed hysterically. "What an echo!"

Joe put his hands in his lap. The noise had hurt his ears, and he was surprised no lights went on in the house.

"Well, come on, Joe," Hippie said coolly. "Finish your lap."

Hippie flushed the toilet and nothing happened. He hadn't noticed it not working before, but judging by the pile of shit in the bowl, it hadn't been working for a few days. Gena left when the drugs dried up, but he didn't really mind. Her voice raked against his raw nerves, so it was better that she left. Hippie put the toilet seat down and sat on it. Across the narrow walkway, the sink sat dry. The soap scum in the shower's drain was hard and cracked.

He leaned forward and turned the faucet, but nothing came out. Standing once more, he braced himself against the sink and held his head low. His mouth was dry. Weeks of shavings stuck to the sink's basin like too much pepper. A sliver of Lava soap was stuck in the bristles of his toothbrush. He ran his tongue over his teeth.

Stumbling through heaps of towels and trash, he went to the cabinet and reached in. The plastic bag was empty, filled with wadded up bits of saran wrap. He laid the bag on the counter and began to unfold the sheets, licking the fine dust that freckled the clear plastic. His needle was dry and clotted in the bottom of the kitchen sink, which had also dried up.

Sunlight filtered through the plastic blinds. They were cracked in the middle from incessant peeking; Hippie stuck two fingers between the slats and peered through. The dirt road leading to the camper was clear save for the Cadillac. The noises of the highway carried over but were dimmed by the hum of summer locusts. Hippie paced the length of the camper—about four yards. The phone rang. He nearly tripped over his own legs leaping to pick it up.

"Hello?" he said. "Hello?"

The dial tone thrummed in the receiver.

"Goodbye," he said.

The lunchtime crowd was settled into wooden booths inside the Washita Café, and the waitresses finally had a minute to themselves. The bell above the glass door jangled as Gena pushed it open with her hip. She leaned against the newspaper box and tugged a pack of Virginia Slims from her shorts' pocket. Hippie's Cadillac glinted in the sun. It had been there when her mom dropped her off at work, but she hadn't seen him in nearly a month. She bent down and checked her lipstick in the side mirror. She smiled to herself, taking a measured drag on her cigarette. If Hippie was up for leaving his place, she guessed he was back on his feet. She'd been feeling a little low lately. She expected to see him at any moment, and she wanted to make him miss her.

"You're golden, baby," she said. She checked her teeth, licking them clean and smacking her lips. She ran her manicured nails through her hair.

Main Street was lined with cars baking in the midday heat. She held her hand over her eyes and scanned the sidewalks. The end of the street tapered to a wavering mirage in the heat. A patrol car came through the wave and turned into the alley that ran between the café and the pawnshop. Gena stuffed her hands in her pockets and fingered the crank she'd wrapped in foil. She recognized the car's driver as Radar Ralph, a cop who came in most days for coffee. Relaxing a little, she allowed herself to pause.

Radar Ralph was just past middle age, and he grunted as he stepped out of the patrol car and hoisted himself from the seat. His mustache dripped down the sides of his mouth past his chin, and the curled tips rose outward like a bird's wings as he smiled at Gena, adjusting his black leather belt.

"Afternoon, Ralph," Gena said. "Coffee, black?"

Radar Ralph rested his hand on his gun. His wide-brim, standard-issue hat sat back on his head, driving an angry crease into his brow. "Not today, thanks." He rolled his shoulders. "I'm here on business today."

Gena's neck prickled, and she forced a smile. "Uh-huh, and what's that?"

"Just your standard traffic complaint. That car right there's been parked since last night, and this is a two-hour parking zone," he said. "Yes, ma'am, I'd say we'll have to tow it in. Abandoned vehicle and all. You know whose it is?"

She shook her head. "Nah, never seen it before."

His boots clacked against the cement as he came around the back of the Cadillac. "Well, yeah, me neither. It's a fat ticket, alright. There's gotta be a full report—"

"They must be real busy down at the station, huh?" Gena said. "When you're done, come on in, and I'll get you a coffee." The bells jingled as she opened the door. The rabble of the crowd drifted outside. "My break's up," she said with an exaggerated sigh. "Bye, Ralph!"

"Take it easy, girl," Radar Ralph said.

It was Tuesday, and the bar was nearly empty. Joe nursed a beer while Carl drank down tumblers of gin. The bartender dozed on a stool in the corner, one eye barely open. The jukebox was between records, and the half a dozen men there didn't want to waste a quarter on it.

"I seem to remember you being a whiskey man," Joe said. He'd shown up between his split shift at the Purina factory. His skin, hair, and clothes smelled like wet dog food. The clock over the bar read 6:30; he had another half hour to kill.

"Funny thing, Joe," Carl said, "I was a whiskey man, but my mom can't get enough of this shit. It's all she buys."

Joe lit a cigarette. Someone finally put on a record. They picked Journey.

"When'd you get back in town? Haven't seen you since you jumped bail in '83," Joe said.

Carl snorted and slapped the bar. The bartender started awake and looked his way. Carl motioned for another gin.

"That was Old Carl. New Carl has a parole officer." The bartender brought over the gin. "Been back since spring. Staying at Mama's. She's getting old, so I think she likes the company." He drank half the tumbler in one swig. "I haven't seen anybody from the old days. Looks like the whole place's cleared out."

"Can't make a dollar to save your life anymore, that's why," Joe said.

"Yeah, guess so," Carl said. He finished his drink and put the glass with the others. "Hell, I guess Robbie—I mean, Hippie—I guess he even lit outta here. Haven't heard hide or hair of the bastard."

Joe tapped his cigarette over the ashtray. Smoke hung heavy in the air.

"Don't be so sure about that, Carl," Joe said and lit a second cigarette with the first. "He might just as soon be at the bottom of Crowder Lake."

"What makes you say that?" Carl asked. The Journey record flipped over. "Mama said he was over at some Eagle City rig."

"The rigs are dry, man," Joe said. "None of us been on a rig in ages. I saw Hip a while back and something wasn't right with him. He wouldn't let me in on it, but he was strung out as hell." Joe chuckled harshly. "He makes for a goofy ass crankster."

"Old Carl would've been sad as hell," Carl said, "hearing you talk like that."

Joe laughed. "And what does New Carl think?"

"New Carl would like another gin."

CARRION

Tennessee cut the tongue out of Pop's boot to get the thing off. Blood had seeped through two pairs of socks. At the sight of blood, Jonathan, his husky, whimpered and snapped her jaws. Tennessee shooed her away. She listened, but he had to tie her puppies to his pack to keep them from licking Pop's boot.

Dark blue and black bruises splintered up Pop's calf. His skin was hot, and Pop cried out when Tennessee cut the sock. A bone, thin and graceful like a bird's wing, reached out like a hatchling beginning its escape. Like he'd been taught, Tennessee bathed his father's foot in the isopropyl alcohol he carried. His father screamed then, a scream that startled him, the high whine of a dying animal, before reeling back in the dirt. The puppies yipped along, excited. He bound the foot in strips of white cloth that bloomed burgundy.

His father breathed for a few days more—wet sickly breaths, unaccepting of water or food. Tennessee kept himself awake by pinching his eyelids and pricking beneath his fingernails with his knife, Pop's bow and quiver on his left. Jonathan lay on his right, growling softly, her puppies suckling noisily. At night, the forest came alive around them, the chirps and howls of the wild circling, waiting.

Pop died about sunrise, just as the morning glow washed over the trees and wooded peaks. In time with the changing of the season, the oak and hickory trees cut a river of burnt gold across the mountains. A tendril of smoke sought out the sky from down in the valley. Probably hunters, Tennessee thought. The time was right for them, and they were the only ones arrogant enough to leave a fire burning. They would stick by the creek, most likely, where the soapberry trees snaked alongside its banks.

The night's siege had ended, and now Tennessee broke up the soil with his hunting knife before laying it aside to scrape away the loose earth. He dug like he'd watched Pop dig. He dug until his fingers ached. He dug until the dirt began to cut into his hands. He knew he was strong, but he could be stronger. He knew from watching the tourists that drove them up the mountain every summer that he was stronger, taller, and faster than their boys, but Pop was a tree of a man, nearly twenty hands high. The hole had to be big.

The wind tore across the terraced camp, shuddering pine needles from their branches. A few pine cones clattered to the ground, and the puppies tried out their barks on them. Tennessee stopped digging, his fingers cramped like spades. The puppies were too loud, not like Jonathan, who knew better.

Maybe they're hungry, Tennessee thought. His own stomach turned, and he felt its emptiness for the first time in days. His father carried the food—too heavy for a boy, he'd said—and Tennessee opened the pack with dirty hands. The tourists were scarce this year, or they made themselves scarce to the campers, Tennessee didn't know. Pop chose their routes and had only just begun teaching him the winding circuit they used. The pack held just a few cans, leftovers, things like soups or chowder, a few mini tins of beans, and about twenty pounds of cured venison they'd just picked up from one of their old camps a few days east. Tennessee broke off a chunk of it and sucked on it until it was soft. He opened one of the mini tins and dumped it on the ground in front of the puppies. It was beans and hot dogs, something the tourists never seemed to run out of, and a meal Tennessee hated. The beans were mushy and sweet, the meat too soft. The puppies scrambled over one another trying to outdo themselves, smearing the sugared sauce onto their paws and muzzles. One puppy yelped as another bit its ear, tripping over its own tether.

The venison settled uneasily in his stomach, and he took a drink from the water jug tethered to the straps of Pop's pack. He drank in long, loud gulps, something Pop would have never allowed. More water than just enough to wet your throat was a pleasure, a luxury taken after a long day and a good meal. Tennessee took another drink, grateful that Pop had died with his eyes closed.

He pulled out another can from the pack: There was some writing on the label, a red banner above a picture of steaming yellow soup in a bowl with blue trim. Tennessee recognized some of the letters, like the *e, n,* and *s* from his name. With his knife, he whittled a hole in the can's top and drank from it. The soup was salty and thick, with a hint of cream that reminded him of the powdered milk they had when he was little. He covered the half-empty can with a cloth and set it in the nook of a loblolly pine to save for later. The puppies began to lick one another's paws and faces for the last bit of beans.

When the puppies were born, Tennessee helped Jonathan along when the fourth and final puppy got stuck. The fourth puppy was fat, much fatter than the others, and when it finally eased from Jonathan, it was clear that the pup was dead. Its sac was filled with water, and the puppy was bloated. Tennessee wondered if the baby in Dead Ma's belly would have come out the same. Tennessee buried the dead pup, but by the next morning, the pup was gone. He hadn't buried it deep enough.

Pop always said a body's got to be buried at least five feet down: Any less and something's bound to dig it up. Tennessee was too young to dig when Ma died, but he watched. He watched Pop scoop away the loam with his wide, thick hands. He watched Pop undress her, peeling her canvas coat from stiff shoulders, tugging off jeans she'd lifted that spring. He watched her big, round belly, squishy now, not hard like before. He sat next to the grave holding Jonathan's neck. He'd named her that after a story Ma liked to tell. She was buried seven winters ago beneath a Woods' rose bush. Pop buried her on the shortest day of the year.

These puppies, now nearly six weeks strong, didn't look quite like Jonathan had as a pup. Their bodies were smaller, longer, and Pop said they were likely coyote pups. He'd wanted to kill them straight off, but Tennessee begged to keep them. He imagined a pack of hunting dogs, trailing alongside them as they crisscrossed the mountains. He imagined himself leading the pack, their alpha.

His back against the tree, he flexed his fingers until his joints began to move properly again. Jonathan came up from behind and nuzzled his neck with her wet snout; she'd wandered to the creek, probably. He scratched her jaw and pressed his face into her neck. He reached into the pack and got her a bit of venison. She tossed it between her jaws before swallowing it whole, and she pressed her nose against Tennessee's palm. He gave her a second piece.

If it weren't for Pop's body lying between two towering post oaks, their camp would've been nice. The little clearing was on high ground with good visibility, couched against the mountain where the grade steepened. For a holdover camp, it was perfect. For a grave, it'd do. But he couldn't stay here through the winter: The wind would strip the tops of the trees before spring, and there wasn't any cover in case of snow or rain. No, he couldn't stay. Tennessee rubbed his palms together, trying to stop their tingling.

He squatted next to the meager hole he'd dug and then, when his ankles began to quake, he got on his knees. He fell into a rhythm with it, driving the knife into the dirt with his left hand, digging methodically with his right. There was a power in the pattern, and with each stab, he drove the knife to its hilt in the dirt. About a foot down, the sandy soil gave way to a soft clay, and it was cold to the touch.

The puppies whined against their tether, and Tennessee kept digging.

The shadow of a turkey buzzard flickered through the trees. Tennessee stopped and watched for the bird's shadow to pass over them again. The thought of a turkey buzzard's gnarled, red head snapping into Pop's belly made him shake. He clenched his fists and kept digging.

By evening, he'd managed a sort of foxhole, nearly waist-deep and about half as long as he needed, but he had to stop for the night. His hands were cracked, and the cracks were caked with clay. The sun had already begun to sink behind what Pop called Mother Lode Mountain. It wasn't the largest peak in the range, but it was closest to a couple of waterfalls, so it was popular with the tourists. In the high season during the summer, they'd cut a path through a few scattered campgrounds, taking what they needed. Mother Lode Mountain tourists brought all kinds of things: RVs, generators, clothes, blankets, canned food, tools. They had enough to never miss a few things here and there, Pop said.

Jonathan, too, had come from the tourists. In the story Ma liked to tell, Jonathan was a boy born into the wrong life, a life built around things. As he grew, he began to see how the people around him were bent and twisted by their things, and he cast himself out and learned to live high in the mountains, in the purest air of all. Tennessee remembered how her voice lilted when the boy made it to the mountaintop. Tennessee's Jonathan was a little thing when Pop brought her back to camp. She had been left alone, tied to an iron stake, Pop said. Tourists didn't know what to do with such a beautiful dog. She would be wasted on them.

Tennessee took the can of soup down from the tree and emptied it, dumping out the last of it for the puppies. Jonathan perked her ears at him, whining, so he used the knife to saw off a chunk of the deer meat. The piece he gave her was bigger than the last, and he knew it'd keep her busy for a while at least. "Stay, girl," he told her. He needed to rinse the cans out so as not to draw any more attention to their camp, and he felt better knowing that Jonathan would be near Pop's body.

He tucked the soup can under his arm and picked up the mini tin, ducking under a low branch to circle back to the thin deer trail. There were rules to pinching from the tourists: never more than one thing per tourist, never the same camp twice in a season, cover your tracks. Part of covering your tracks meant washing out the cans and stripping the labels. That way, Pop said, the tourists couldn't prove nothing. The creek ran a little more than a quarter mile west, and Tennessee hurried, keeping one eye on the path and the other on the rapidly setting sun. He came out of the trees on a slope and took small steps through the high grass.

The soup sloshed in his stomach. It felt as if his mouth were coated thick with it. It had been stupid of him to eat it so quickly. He'd been greedy. If he were honest, he'd admit it never sat well with him, the canned stuff. But for the seconds it took to eat it, it was the best thing he ever tasted. He hoped he wouldn't throw up.

He cut through a thicket of soapberry trees and came out on the south end, at the creek. The water level was low, the creek's silt banks bordering the narrow pass. A bright green bullet casing lay in a clump of grass, and Tennessee picked it up. The casing was cold, and he tossed it into the stream, watching as it bobbed like a cheap cork downstream. A shameful way to hunt, bullets.

He tapped the sand with the toe of his boot until he found a spot that didn't sink. Crouching over the creek, he ran the can under the cool stream. Once the cans were rinsed, he peeled the labels off and crushed them into pulpy balls, tossing each one into the water. Minnows swam near the surface, picking at the paper as it floated downstream. He set the cans on the bank and scrubbed his hands. He left a murky current, but the coolness soothed the sharp ache that seeped out of his hands. The clay had worked itself into the swoops and whorls of his palms; he shook the water from his hands.

The creek, its current no longer broken, reflected the purple sky as dusk set in. Somewhere in the vast expanse of pine and oak, a coyote howled. Further out, other coyotes joined the chorus, and their calls reverberated across the range. With every round, some were closer, others further away. The pack circled. Tennessee shook the cans out and forced them into his jacket pockets and headed back through the thicket.

When he was little, Pop told a story to keep him close. It wasn't like Ma's story about Jonathan. Instead, Pop's story was about a man who wore a long coat. The man lived in their mountains, and he skirted the tourists with enviable ease. He ran with the deer, the elk, the coyotes, the bobcats, and even the bears. For all intents and purposes, he wasn't a man at all. He followed the tourists' trails, and when he felt like it, when he found one he wanted to punish, he'd pick them off. Poof.

You've gotta be smarter, Pop said. You've got to stay close to camp.

The high grass rustled further up the slope, and a howl rang out, so close that Tennessee felt it in his chest. He pushed on, cursing himself. He'd taken too long; he'd dawdled. Now it was night and he ran, his footfalls in time with his heartbeat. The cans clanged inside his pocket. In the daylight, he knew the path, but under the thick shroud of darkness, the deer trail was just a sliver of sand, barely traceable. But he did know this path, and he let his muscles lead, quick strides that left behind heavy boot prints.

Cover your tracks, Pop said. Stay close to camp.

You've got to bury a body five feet down, Pop said. Or something's liable to dig it up.

He nearly fell as he burst through the pines, but he righted himself and surveyed their camp. Pop was laid up next to the hole, his arms at his sides. His pack was open, and the ground was strewn with shreds of paper. Jonathan was backed up against her puppies, who were scrambling excitedly over Tennessee's pack, their tether tangled around their bellies. She cocked an ear at him and snarled into the dark. He went to her and scratched the scruff of her neck.

"S'alright," Tennessee said quietly. "Done good."

She tossed her heavy head beneath his hand and kept her nose pointed west. He went to Pop's pack, tucking the empty cans in the front pocket. He didn't need to open the big pocket to know the venison was gone. His mouth was dry as he swept the paper scraps into a pile. He hadn't tied up the main pocket; that was stupid. That was so simple, so sensible, as to have never been codified into law. Pop never left his pack untended. The bulging moss-green pack was his shadow, and now it occurred to Tennessee why. His eyes went hot, but he grit his teeth, grateful again that Pop had died with his eyes closed.

The howls quieted for the moment. Jonathan's ears were tucked flush against her head, her teeth bared. The coyotes were silent, but they were there, just beyond the trees. Tennessee could hear the gnashing of their jaws as they ate his venison. He swallowed air as if that would fill him. He had to keep digging.

Tennessee wrapped his hands in the white cloth and grabbed his knife from beneath the empty pack. He kneeled by the foxhole, his breath rattling as he stabbed at the dirt. The knife broke the soil again and again, and he drove it deeper with each stroke. The cracks in his hands opened, rubbing raw against the coarse cloth, but he kept digging. He wished for a shovel, like the one Pop had taken to bury Ma. Pop left that shovel at a campsite.

Don't carry what you don't need, Pop said.

His stomach lurched, and he tamped down the urge to heave. His mouth was wet. He swallowed and kept digging.

Miles down the ridge, a mountain lion screamed. Its shrill, plaintive cry mimicked that of a woman. Tennessee paused, listening: The scream had silenced the other creatures lurking in the night. The quiet was uncomfortable, the only sounds being the scrape and brush of the knife in the soil, the sweep of the dirt. The quiet was like a blindfold. When he and Pop stalked deer, the moment before the arrow's slick release, the moment before the arrow pierced its breast was quiet: In that moment of stillness, the deer knew.

He crawled into the hole on his knees and, leaving the knife suspended in the side of the hole, used his hands to break up the clay wall. Closer to the surface, the dirt came away easily. Worms and grubs wriggled, reaching out into the air, struggling to right themselves as he swept them into the loose piles of dirt. He'd eaten worms when he was little, curious at first and then just because he liked it. Pop clapped his ears for that.

Men don't eat worms, Pop said.

He kept digging. Jonathan pawed at the hole's edge. The mountain lion screamed again. The moon climbed overhead, illuminating him through a gap in the trees. He kept digging.

The coyotes started up again, and he dug faster, urgently. They circled as they had before.

We know you're there, they seemed to say.

Tennessee's arms quaked when he took up the knife again. The wind chilled him, and on its tail, he caught a rancid, hot scent. With another gust it was gone, but he knew that if he could smell it, the coyotes had always smelled it: They liked it. Tennessee wiped the sweat from his brow, and he felt the dirt smear across his face.

He kept digging.

As the dark sky began to pale, birds began to wake, and a bobwhite whistled in the pine. The hole was deep and, exhausted, Tennessee found that when he stood, his head was just below the earth's surface. He could almost extend his arms down the hole's length, but it was painful to try. The bobwhite whistled.

The bobwhite is the man in the long coat's messenger, Pop said.

Jonathan began to growl. On his tiptoes, Tennessee saw her crouching low against the ground. From between the pines, a gray coyote slunk into the camp. Jonathan snapped her jaws and barked. She backed up against her puppies.

The mountain is more afraid of you than you are of it, Pop said. The man in the long coat isn't afraid of anything.

Tennessee jumped and tried to hook his elbows over the hole's lip, but the ground gave way, and he fell back hard on his tailbone. He got up and tried again. He fell. He screamed, grabbed a handful of clay, and lobbed it out of the hole. He heard it clatter into the grass. Still, Jonathan barked and snarled.

Panic gripped his body as he heard the wet snap of jaws. He groped blindly for the knife. He found it and held it tightly in his left hand. He jumped, jabbing it into the earth, and tried to pull himself out. The effort made him cry out. He kicked at the clay, finding a foothold and propelling himself up. He pulled himself out of the hole and turned, crouching low with his knife in front of him.

Jonathan was in a frenzy, her puppies crying between her hind legs. Two coyotes were on Pop, one gnawing his blackened foot, the other tearing at his wide hands. Their muzzles were speckled with dark blood.

Tennessee screamed and charged, swinging the knife in front of him. He caught one on the shoulder. It yelped and jumped back. The larger of the two crouched low and lunged, and Tennessee stabbed at it, the effort of his swing spinning him on his feet as he missed. The big one sank its teeth into his calf. He tried to shake the beast off, but it held its grip. He slashed its nose, and the coyote released him, shaking its snout as it retreated.

The coyotes didn't run, but slunk away just as they'd come. They were confident: The sun was rising, but it would set again. Tennessee brought his legs to his chest and wrapped his arms around himself. Jonathan licked his hand, her puppies yipping excitedly. He swallowed a sob. He clenched his jaw until it throbbed.

Crying is a waste of resources, Pop said.

Tennessee crawled to the pack and rummaged for the isopropyl alcohol. Rolling up the cuff of his pants, the bite didn't look too bad, considering how his leg throbbed, how he could feel it throbbing in his ears. He counted seven good puncture wounds, two of which bit into the muscle of his calf, but none so wide or deep as to need stitches. When he poured the alcohol over it, he thought that he could hear his skin burning, searing into his leg. There was just enough white cloth left to wrap the worst of his leg. He wrapped it as tightly as he could.

He took a shaky breath and looked to Pop. The bandage on his foot was torn, chunks of flesh ripped away in thick, ragged pieces. His thumb was gone. Tennessee pressed his palms into the grass. Pop's face was slack.

The bobwhite whistled.

Tennessee rubbed his eyes with his fists. His knuckles were wet. He stood, careful, and lifted Pop's ankles. It startled him how much meat looked like meat. The flesh of a dead man wasn't much different than that of a deer.

He dragged Pop to the side of the hole. The body's stiffness was fading, and Tennessee sat him up, his arms barely reaching around Pop's chest. Tennessee pressed his face into Pop's shoulder. Pop's jacket smelled of dirt and smoke, but the smell of iron lingered faintly. Tennessee rocked a little, back and forth, and let out a shallow breath. Gingerly, he crooked Pop's elbow and tugged his arm out of the sleeve. He did the same with the other arm, careful with Pop's mangled hand. He scooted out from behind Pop, pulling the jacket off. Pop slumped forward.

He flipped Pop into the hole. He heard the crack of something inside Pop. He looked down into the hole and saw Pop, contorted oddly in a kind of squat, his legs twisted beneath him. Tennessee's own leg throbbed, but he tried to push it out of his mind. Kneeling beside the hole, the grave, Tennessee began to fill it, scooping heavy handfuls of dirt over his father's body. The splash of the dirt sounded like a hard, sporadic rain.

The sun was in the center of the sky when he finished. He collapsed beside the grave, hungry and exhausted, and tried to catch his breath. Jonathan lay next to him, and he ruffled her fur. The puppies slept next to the pack in a pile of soft fur the color of wet sand.

When his sweat turned cold and the throbbing in his leg calmed to a cruel ache, he opened a can of beans and took a small bite. The food disturbed his empty stomach, and he dumped half of the can onto the ground for Jonathan. The husky lapped it up hungrily, finishing it just as the puppies woke and tousled over one another, eager to join her. Tennessee counted the cans: two tins of beans and two others, both with pictures of orange soup on the label. The dirt that crusted his arms cracked as he pulled himself up.

It would freeze soon, Tennessee knew. The cave Pop pointed them toward was still five days south, more with a busted calf. He brought the canteen to his lips and drank until he heard the water sloshing in his belly.

The puppies played, still tangled in their makeshift leash.

They will starve, Tennessee knew.

He twirled his knife's tip in the dirt. He could hunt. Pop's bow was a little big for him, but he could manage. But that would take time. The tourists were gone, and the few hunters that still roamed the valleys were dangerous.

Hunters hung the heads of their kills on walls in painted lodges, Pop said. They killed for the sake of the kill. We are not like them.

No, there wasn't time to hunt.

He crawled to the puppies. Gently, he untethered them, unlooping the rope from around their fat paws. They mewled and tumbled over one another, happy to be free of their restraints. They nipped at his fingers.

He took one in his hands, a boy pup, and rubbed the soft felt of its ears. He pulled at the scruff of its neck. He drew his knife across its throat; it fell limp in his hands as its blood pumped out of its body, seeping into the dirt. Jonathan cried in short yips. She barked. She pawed at the ground, her tail between her legs.

Tennessee's mouth was wet. He laid the dead puppy on the ground and slit it down the middle. It was warm, the puppy, and its insides were warm as Tennessee reached into the animal. A little stomach. A liver. The puppy wasn't much of a thing.

He looked at Jonathan, and he saw a sadness in her eyes. He looked away.

He would skin the puppy. He would start a fire. He would harvest what little meat the puppy had. He'd be on the move by nightfall. It would freeze soon.

The bobwhite whistled again, and a mockingbird returned its call. The bobwhite was silent.

WHAT'S YOURS AND WHAT'S MINE

LeAnn knew she was hot when her boobs came in. She'd always thought she was pretty, not gorgeous, but nice enough: not too tall or too short, thin where it mattered, thick where it didn't. Her hair was mousy brown, and her skin wasn't too bad. But her boobs are what really brought her up a notch. She could tell by the way the men hanging around outside the Blue Room looked at her when she passed on her way to school. They'd whistle and tell her how she'd like it if she'd just give them the chance to give it to her. She pretended to hate it, flipping them the bird behind her back, but really she focused on swinging her hips just right, with just the right amount of sass to let them know she was hot shit. That always made them howl.

LeAnn's mama was half crippled from a nasty car wreck, and from her rocking chair on the porch, she saw the way the older boys in the trailer park followed after LeAnn like fleas on a dog. Her mama knew what it was like to be beautiful. She'd had her own rotating cast of boyfriends with nice cars and custom suits, but after the wreck laid her up, she stopped dating altogether. Nobody wants to date a fat cripple on disability. When she saw the first heads turning, she sat her daughter down and told her there was no reason to give the milk away for free. "If you're going to give it, and believe me, they're going to want it," she said, "just make sure you get yours first. That was my biggest mistake." LeAnn's mama rolled her eyes as she said then, "I just gave it all away."

So when a sophomore asked to see LeAnn's tits at a football game, she met him beneath the bleachers at halftime and lifted her sweater for five bucks and a lift home. Sitting in front of her trailer later that night, he offered another five if he let him touch them. She talked him up to an even twenty if he could go under her bra, and she lifted her sweater again. His hands were cold and scratchy, but it didn't feel like anything. After a while she thought he'd gone long enough and besides, she was bored of it, so she pushed his hands away and tugged her sweater down. He thanked her as she got out of his truck, and she flipped him off. The sophomore must've told his friends anyway because it was just a couple of days before others started calling her at home after school, wondering if they could give her a ride, too. "C'mon, LeAnn," they said, "why not me?" And she went, more often than not, putting up a big show before giving in. She learned quick that the longer she put them off, the more they wanted to give her. Five and ten dollars here and there, nothing below the waist (though a junior guy made her touch his dick once, but he looked like he felt bad about it when he took her to Dairy Queen after).

Her mama saw her with money, even though she pretended not to at first. It was a couple of months before she asked LeAnn where it was coming from. "Friends," LeAnn said, because it wasn't really a lie, no, not really. Her mama snorted and turned back to stirring some noodles in a pot on the stove. "Well, your *friends* need to start kicking in around here," her mama said. "And ten percent to God, too," she added, but she didn't hold LeAnn to that part.

She'd just turned fifteen when she started hanging around the beer bars down by the interstate. The gawky college dropout who lived with his grandma a few trailers down took her there, and afterwards they fucked on the backseat of his grandma's

Town Car in the parking lot. It was her first time, and he gave her fifty dollars and bought her a peach Bartles & Jaymes. He'd brought the condom, and she was surprised at how easy it was, fucking him. He was more than happy to do the work, and he finished quickly. He tossed the condom out the window and sighed, "You don't look fifteen." He said he would take her out again, but he didn't call. She pouted about it for a few days, sure, but he was just some dropout with no job anyway. The men at the bars had liked her, and it was easy enough to hitch a ride down there, most times for nothing more than some old farmer peeking down her shirt.

The guys at the beer bars had jobs and their own cars; some of them even had their own trucks with a bed and little kitchenette in the cab. They were mostly truckers, oil riggers, and day laborers (white ones—the Mexicans had their own bar out by the old rodeo grounds). The boom was on then, and pretty much every man she met either worked on the rigs, built the rigs, or hauled parts for the rigs back and forth across the state. LeAnn had never left Custer County, and sometimes it was nice when one of the truckers would talk about some place she'd never seen, like Galveston or Little Rock. But mostly she liked that they had thick wallets that left imprints in their back pockets. After the first few, she started to know who and what she liked: the younger ones, mostly riggers, tanned and tightly muscled from their work. They smelled like axle grease, and their hands were rough no matter how gently they touched her. They wanted to make her cum and sometimes she did, but otherwise she let them think she did because she liked the way they seemed so proud of themselves. She hated some of the others, especially the ones who told her she reminded them of their daughters.

LeAnn hated school, too. She was always tired, and she felt the other girls sizing her up out of the corners of their eyes.

She knew they all thought she was a trailer trash slut, but their boyfriends and their brothers hadn't seemed to mind so much, right? Most of those girls she'd known since kindergarten, like Sarah, who peed her pants on the sixth grade zoo trip, or Cathy, who got caught with her pants around her ankles on the playground back in third grade. But they still talked about her. LeAnn the slut. In the bathroom one day, she overheard Cathy and another girl whispering about her. They said she'd gotten AIDS from balling faggots, which didn't even make sense in the first place. She played sick for a few days—where would she even go if she wanted to skip?—before she told her mama she wasn't going back. Her mama didn't like that, but LeAnn wouldn't budge on it. Besides, her mama didn't get a say so long as she was getting hers, too.

It was nice spending the days at home. In the late morning and afternoons, LeAnn and her mama watched the soaps together. Their favorite was *General Hospital,* but they watched them all: *Days, All My Children, One Life to Live.* All those people living such complicated lives in faraway towns with gazebos in well-kept parks; nothing like Erath or Pleasant Valley Trailer Park. In fact, LeAnn would've bet money they didn't even have trailer parks in places like Salem or Port Charles. On commercial breaks, LeAnn would make them eggs-in-the-hole and refill their coffee mugs with the watery instant coffee her mama liked. They just couldn't get enough of Luke and Laura, the Romeo and Juliet of *General Hospital.* Things had started out so rough for them, but LeAnn watched their wedding with tears running down her face. It was hard to be in love, wasn't it?

After a while, LeAnn felt like she needed to get out of the house. She applied for a straight job bar-backing at the Blue Room, the only bar actually in town. The owner, Steve, didn't care that she was underage, so long as she cut the neck out of her T-shirt and worked his shifts. His other bartenders were two old lady barflies, and they didn't seem to like LeAnn much, but tips went up when she was around, so Steve kept her shifts to himself. Her shifts were short, usually eight to midnight, which left enough time for her to hitch a ride to the beer bars once the Blue Room closed up. With her tips (which she suspected Steve of overestimating, but she couldn't complain), she made the same as if she spent the whole night at the beer bars, but with half the hassle. And the shots the Blue Room regulars bought her didn't hurt.

From the start, it was obvious Steve had a thing for her. He would cop a feel of her ass as she refilled the ice locker. Brush his hand across her crotch reaching for a bottle like it was an accident. It wasn't a big deal—he looked like he was cute once in the bar's patchy lighting. She'd been there about two weeks when he asked her to suck him off. It was just after closing, and he'd made her a rum and Coke with the top-shelf rum. She'd already figured out that she didn't like rum, but she drank the rum and Coke anyway while he counted out her tips. He gave her seventy-five dollars from the jar, nearly all of it. It was rude not to return favors.

It was kind of a regular thing, sucking off Steve. He liked to drive her home after, dropping her off a few blocks away. She knew he'd figured out her gig at the beer bars, but it wasn't any of his business. He wasn't exactly sweeping her off her feet. Probably a month or so in, he said he'd give her 200 bucks a week to stop hanging around the beer bars. She laughed, and his face scrunched up. He slapped the bar towel over his shoulder and pressed her against the bar, his hips grinding into her ass. "It's not safe out there," he said. He wrapped his hand around her chin and pulled her back toward him. "You're too pretty for a beer bar." His grip tightened for a second, and then he let go, unpinning her. She watched him adjust the bulge in his pants.

She took her time pouring two fingers of Burnett's Peach Vodka into a tumbler. She liked the sweet stuff that kicked. It was fun to watch Steve squirm. Just a second ago he'd been all macho, and now he was holding a towel over his boner. She swirled the vodka in the glass. It smelled like nail polish remover mixed with peach gummy candy. Knocking it back in one swig, she slammed the glass down on the bar. "You just want to fuck me," she said. She grinned and pushed her shoulders back. The burn in her stomach made her feel ten feet tall. "C'mon, say it."

"I can take care of you," Steve said. He'd sweat through his button-down. "You're just too pretty for a beer bar."

"So long as I get mine," she said. He stared at her a little too long, and it made her itch, not being able to read his face. He should be happy she was even talking to him about this. He took a step toward her, and she flinched, though she tried to cover it by tucking her hair behind her ear. He didn't seem to notice because then his hands were on her hips and her arms were looped around his neck and his tongue was in her mouth. With her legs around his waist, he carried her into the back office and fucked her on the couch. She focused on the sharp line of his jaw, in need of a few days' shave, clenched tight as he fucked her. In the office's yellow fluorescent light, she decided Steve wasn't as cute as she'd thought. His nose and cheeks were ruddy, and he really did sweat too much. He took too long, too, and finished inside her without asking. She'd been stupid not to check for a condom, but the whole thing had gone to her head. The guys at the beer bars always carried their own condoms. She cleaned herself up in the bathroom, and when she was done, Steve hadn't come out of the office and he'd closed the door. She opened the register and lifted the cash drawer, counting out fifteen 20 dollar bills from the paper-clipped stack. She put the money in her purse and walked home.

True to his word, Steve was there every Saturday night after with a rubber-banded roll of twenties. He always put the roll in her purse before he took her to the back office to fuck her on the couch again. He never mentioned the money she'd taken from the register, so she kept skimming on nights he stayed in his office after they'd fucked. She did tell him she'd cut his dick off if he ever came inside her again, and he laughed, but she swore she could do it. He was no Luke, even if Luke had done terrible things. Steve would just be a background actor in Port Charles, tending bar in a penguin suit. Sometimes she wondered what he did in the office after she left, naked and covered in his own cum, but it was more curiosity than anything else. Facts were that Steve was easy money.

LeAnn's mama didn't like it, though. She said she knew Steve from way back and she didn't like LeAnn spending so much time with him. She brought it up while they were watching the soaps, on a commercial break for discount diapers. "That man ain't your friend," her mama said. She turned down the volume on the brand new television with built-in VCR that LeAnn bought her for Christmas. "He's trying to trap you. He's no friend to you." LeAnn began to gather up their lunch dishes, stacking the plates and cups. Her mama grabbed her wrist and held it tight. "You look at me. You're going to settle? How much do you think you're worth, girl?" So she cut the neck a little deeper on her T-shirt, bought a new pair of Daisy Dukes, and started picking up dates at the Blue Room. The way she figured, Steve was paying her not to hang around the beer bars. He didn't say anything about the Blue Room, and besides, LeAnn's mama was right. Steve wouldn't last. One night, she caught him crying into a bottle of tequila, his accounts' book open in front of him. He couldn't figure out where all his money was going. So he was stupid, too.

Her first dates there were National Guardsmen on their way to some tornado-flattened town. They were a few years older, and one had nice eyes. Steve was pissing her off when they asked her over to their motel, so she said yes and made sure Steve saw her walk out between them. They only had fifty bucks between them, so she ended up just sucking them off before heading back to the Blue Room to finish her shift. Of course, she didn't tell Steve that.

She didn't go for Blue Room regulars: They were mostly old men with tobacco-stained mustaches and swollen, alcoholic noses. She was careful, and she didn't pick up just anybody. She'd watch and wait as the night went on and pick out the types who weren't likely to hang around. There was a former minor league baseball player who didn't take his dip out the entire time and when he came, he whispered, "Over the fence," through his teeth. One was a CO from the prison; he was just sad. Afterwards, he gave her a hundred dollars and asked her to spoon him. She did, but then he started to cry, and she couldn't be there anymore. She missed the oil riggers from the beer bars, but working out of the Blue Room did make for quicker business. And sometimes a cowboy would come by, usually on his way through the rodeo circuit, with hands as tough as leather, and then for the next few days she would imagine he won his class—bull riding, or bronc riding, or whichever— with a fat cash prize. He'd be back through and they'd go on a proper date, to Del Rancho or something. Or he got his head kicked in or his lung stomped through. One of them told her those bulls can weigh as much as 2,000 pounds. Just tragic. They could've been such beautiful boys.

A couple of days after her sixteenth birthday, LeAnn was in the Blue Room, sizing up the Saturday crowd. Steve was already drinking and looked to be nursing a hangover at the same time, so she manned the bar. It was slow for a Saturday, and she was looking forward to Steve passing out so she could close the bar early, get her 200, and go home. The only customers were a couple of bikers holed up in the corner of the bar. They were drinking Budweiser on tap and drinking fast. Their vests said *Dead Rats* on the back over a patch of a poison symbol on top of a rat skull. The young guy who kept getting up for their pitchers had the cleanest vest, with just a patch that read *Prospect* on the back. It was obvious he didn't have any money—a big bear of a man with a heavy, gray beard and a vest covered in patches counted out the bills from a fist-sized roll each time he sent the kid up—but Prospect was kind of cute, and LeAnn was bored. She asked him about the club, what his patch meant (though it wasn't hard to figure out), and made sure to push her boobs up with her arms as she leaned over the bar.

"Never seen y'all around," she offered. "Passing through?"
He handed over exact change and nodded quickly. He glanced back at the table like a rabbit.

"Oh, I don't bite," she said.

The big man yelled something, and the prospect spooked, hurrying back to the table. So much for that. He was just a prospect anyway. She watched them slosh beer into their mugs, draining the pitchers.

She could tell by the way they were talking and laughing that they were talking about her. The big man caught her staring and winked. She pushed her shoulders back and put one hand on her hip, smiling. The big man waved her over and introduced himself as Little John. He was in charge, LeAnn could tell. Not her type, with his big belly stretching over his jeans, but he had a big laugh and a fat stack of bills in his vest. His eyes were running up her body so hard she couldn't help but smirk. Little John ordered tequila shots for the table and one for her, too, and she felt his eyes on her ass as she walked back to the bar. It made her want to laugh, really. Once she'd served the shots and they'd all cheers'd, he handed her a wad of bills with a quick "keep the change" and a pat on the ass. At the register, she realized he tipped her a hundred dollars on an eighteen dollar tab. As much as she'd make putting two hours in at the beer bars made in just a few minutes. When Little John called for more shots, she hiked up her shorts and set up another round.

By closing time, Steve was slumped against the bar, piss drunk, and LeAnn and the Dead Rats were like old friends. On Little John's left were Crystal Pete and Ham, and on his right, Jimmy Pins and the prospect, Manuel. With more than a few shots of tequila in her, LeAnn climbed on Little John's lap and listened to them talk about their bikes, their runs, and their old ladies, all while keeping their glasses full and the cash moving. Crystal Pete told nasty jokes that she pretended to blush at, and even though Manuel didn't seem to talk unless somebody said something to him directly, she caught him staring at her thigh, exposed as it was with Little John practically holding her like a baby in his wide arms. The roll of bills bit into her rib cage.

When the other Rats got up to leave, Little John set her on top of the table and invited her along. "Come party with us," he said. "We like you."

"Oh, Little John," she said. She tapped his arm gently. "Everybody likes me." She laughed. He'd given her five 100 dollar bills by then. "I'm no tease. Let me get my purse." She hopped off of the table and beelined to the back office. Steve was still slumped at the bar. He might be pissed when he woke up, but he could be, for all she cared. With her purse on her shoulder, she popped the register open: No need to leave behind her $200. The ding must've woken him because she turned around and he was blocking the end of the bar, wobbly on his feet. He tried to take a step forward, but he fell straight on his ass, that idiot. He looked ridiculous, his pants slung low enough to show his ass crack, facedown on the rubber floor mats. The front door's bell rang, and Little John filled the frame. "You all right, hon?"

"Yeah, fine, thanks," she said. She stepped over Steve. "I'm just going to lock up. He shouldn't be up for a while."

That really set Steve off. He couldn't even get to his feet, but he managed to roll over and start screaming up a storm about how she couldn't leave, it was Saturday, and how dare she, just another trailer park whore cunt, just like her mama. He'd just gotten that last part out when Little John came in and stomped his chest hard enough to knock the air out of his lungs. Next, Little John's heavy boot crashed into Steve's jaw; a couple teeth skittered across the hardwood.

"You don't talk to women like that," Little John said, the heel of his boot crashing into Steve's knee. Steve had started to cry, or maybe it was just that his nose was broken, but he was really screaming. Then it was Little John, Ham, and Crystal Pete kicking him, too, big, black motorcycle boots coming down on Steve's head and arms and legs. There was a lot of blood, and the smell of it surprised her. She felt almost giddy. No one had the right to talk to her like that—Little John was right. When he offered her the honors, she declined and held onto his arm.

"I think he's done," she said. She locked the door behind her just like she'd promised.

LeAnn spent the next two days partying with the Dead Rats. They had a ton of booze at their clubhouse and she thought, Well, why not. I'm already here. There were more guys there, but she didn't catch all their names. There were other girls, too. LeAnn pretended they didn't exist. They were mostly older than her, what her mama would call "rode hard and put up wet." One of them was a little horsey in the face.

The second night, drunk and stoned, she followed Little John into a bedroom and fucked him. Even through the tequila fog, she remembered that $500 in her purse, and how quickly he came in when Steve was hassling her. Fair was fair. When Crystal Pete came in and asked for sloppy seconds, she let him, because it was only fair, and at some point she knew she'd need a ride home. Crystal Pete was rougher than Little John, but faster to cum. Then it was Ham after Pete finished and then finally Jimmy Pins. She imagined them lining up outside the door, then realized that was probably what they were doing.

Jimmy Pins, being last, stuck around like a boyfriend or something after he was done. He'd probably been a good-looking man once, but his beard was graying and he smelled stale, like old sweat. She was so tired and drunk (and a little sore) that she closed her eyes and listened as he told her about crashing his bike and the pins that held his knee together. "If it weren't for those pins," he said, "I'd have been right there kicking the shit out of that cocksucker motherfucker. No way to treat a woman." She let him wrap his arms around her waist.

Jimmy was gone when she woke up the next morning, but she found Manuel and Little John in the kitchen. Little John and Crystal Pete were nursing beers while Manuel picked up the crushed cans and empty bottles that covered the counters and tables. When he saw her, Little John grinned and threw his arms wide. "There she is," he said. "We were just talking about you."

She smiled and hugged him. "Nothing bad, right?" she said.

"Never." He waved for Manuel to get him another beer, and the prospect did. "We got a rally up in Osage County next weekend. Could use a girl like you on the run. Old ladies will be there, though, so you'd be riding with the prospect." Manuel didn't even look up, he just kept picking up cans. So maybe he was a dead end, but there'd be plenty of other guys like the Rats there. Besides, most of the guys looked like they had old ladies and they still partied. "You can tell your mama you're safe with us. I'll even ask her for permission," Little John said.

"She doesn't get a say in what I do. Why don't you just pick me up Friday?" she said. It embarrassed her, him talking about her mama like that. "But I should probably be getting home."

He laughed his big-bellied laugh and for a second he looked like Santa Claus after a stint in prison. "Sure thing, little sister," he said. "Manuel will drive you home. Wouldn't want your mama to worry."

LeAnn couldn't remember most of the ride out to the clubhouse, so she was surprised it took them nearly an hour to get back to Erath. Without the courage of tequila, the scream of the wind and the way the bike leaned around every curve made her lock her hands around Manuel's waist. Once they got into town, he followed her directions and dropped her off in front of her trailer. Her mama was sitting on the porch smoking, and Manuel even waved at her, though her mama just tapped the ash off her cigarette in his direction. LeAnn told him not to mind her mama and when Manuel said he'd pick her up Friday, she thought it was cute he thought they had a date. She kissed him on the cheek, and his cheek was warm and smooth.

Her mama followed her inside the trailer and just wouldn't shut up about LeAnn being gone so long. "If you were so worried, Mama," LeAnn said, "then why didn't you call the cops?" She started digging through her purse while her mama huffed. "Here," LeAnn said, shoving the $500 Little John gave her across the kitchen table. "I'm getting mine. There's yours," she said.

LeAnn's mama spent the next week saying that Manuel wouldn't show. LeAnn didn't mention what happened at the clubhouse, and the money she made seemed like enough to keep her mama from asking. Five hundred bucks was a lot of money, more than her mama's whole disability check. During the day, they ordered pizza from the gas station takeout place and watched the soaps until *Jeopardy!* came on, and then LeAnn spent the evenings at the beer bars. Word had gotten out about Steve, but none of her friends at the bars seemed bothered by it. She saw a couple of the Blue Room regulars out there that week, but nobody talked about Steve. That had to mean he was fine, and she just went about her business.

On Friday, Manuel showed up like he said he would, and LeAnn was ready with her tightest top, her shortest shorts, and her hair curled, though you couldn't tell with the scarf she'd picked out for the ride to the rally. She let her mama pick the scarf, actually. "Motorcycles don't do any favors for your hair or your ass," her mama said. She didn't come out to the porch, but LeAnn saw her peeking through the blinds as she and Manuel rode away.

They met up with Little John and the other Rats at a truck stop outside of Guthrie. All the other women, the old ladies and the girlfriends, were wearing leather chaps and vests with patches that read *Property of Dead Rats*. For a second, LeAnn felt glaringly out of place. She went to the bathroom in the gas station once the other women were done and touched up her makeup. "You look good," she said into the mirror. "No, better. You look *great*." She blew herself a kiss. So what if she was riding on the back of a prospect's bike.

A couple hours later, she and the Rats she knew and probably thirty other bikers and their girls roared up to the campsite. Her arms and face tingled from the sheer velocity of the ride. It was exhilarating, riding in a pack like that, everything drowned out by the grumble of motorcycle engines. She saw a movie once where some bikers threw chains behind them at drivers who didn't respect their ride. She wondered if the Rats had ever done anything like that.

The men disappeared almost as soon as they'd parked their bikes. Manuel helped a couple of other prospects set up tents while LeAnn sulked in the shade. She hadn't known they'd be staying overnight; she'd need a payphone to call her mama. And she only brought the one outfit. The old ladies had already set themselves up near the water pump, and she thought for sure they were sneaking stares at her. Whatever. There were a couple girls who looked her age by the tents, but they didn't bother to introduce themselves either. Bored, she left the campsite and wandered the alleys around the grounds: beer and burger stands, a pop-up trailer where a man with an Iron Cross tattooed under his eye swore he'd seen her before. "Last weekend, yeah?" he said. She shook her head. "You sure? At the Nation rally?"

It seemed like every man she passed had a woman on his arm already. She wanted a drink, so she had a couple beers courtesy of a Devil's Disciple who was already too drunk to remember his name. She tried to talk him out of some cash, but it turned out he was drinking on credit, so she took that instead. When she had a good buzz on, she circled the grounds again and didn't come up with a single date—not any that didn't want it for free anyhow. She was beginning to get frustrated. She hadn't seen anyone in a Rats' vest in hours, and she began to miss the security of the beer bars. Those drunks weren't loaded, but they were always there. Dependable. There had to be someone at this goddamn rally who could see what a catch she was.

At the center of the grounds, an open clearing was rigged with lights and speakers, and LeAnn hovered at the edge of the crowd as the emcee's voice boomed into the tree line. Beneath a string of Christmas lights, a wire was strung between two thin trees about a school bus length apart. In the middle, a second wire hung down. Near the front of the crowd, she recognized the Dead Rats' patch and started forcing her way through the crowd. Someone copped a feel of her boobs, then a hand on her ass. She kept pushing until she reached Little John and the others. The ground was a little muddy (from beer, it smelled like) and she slipped, grabbing onto Ham's arm as she fell. Before she got to her feet, he'd already passed her off to Manuel. The woman with Ham was probably his wife. Her shorts were ripped on the left seam, but she was grateful Manuel at least kept her out of the mud.

The emcee hooked a hot dog to a hook on the end of the second string. "Who will be," he started, "this year's Deep Throat Queen?" The crowd around her whooped and hollered. "And the winner gets $1,000!" The shouts got louder, and hands were pushing her forward until she was nearly thrown out into the clearing with a couple other girls, one who had on a pair of assless chaps. LeAnn's tongue was dry from the heat and the beers, but she knew she'd heard right: a $1,000. She kept her shoulders back and her hand on her hip as the emcee explained the rules: The crowd would nominate a biker for each girl; they'd each get three chances on the back of the bike to catch the hot dog in their mouths as their biker drove; they'd have different bikers, but the bike would be the same, a Harley that looked like it'd been through hell. The girl who caught the most dog after her turns would be that year's Deep Throat Queen.

The men in the crowd were rowdy. They shouted and punched the air, clamoring over one another, jostling. LeAnn sized up the other girls. There was Assless Chaps, some bleach blond with a bruised tooth, and a leggy redhead. The leggy redhead had some height on her, but the bleach blond was chunky. Assless Chaps was harder to read, but the emcee chose her to go first, so LeAnn didn't have much time to overthink it. The crowd picked her biker, a guy with a mullet and a scar splitting his lip, and he straddled the old Harley with her behind him. The crowd cheered again when the emcee dipped the hot dog in a jar of spicy mustard, thick, yellow strings of the stuff slinging off into the grass. But the guy with the mullet must've been drunk or something, because the bike jolted forward and as she leaned back, the bike toppled over, almost in slow motion. A few bikers were quick to lift the bike off them, but it looked like Assless Chaps was burned pretty bad on her leg. Some old lady helped her up, and a prospect moved the bike back to the other side of the clearing. The emcee grinned at the crowd with a shrug. He thumped the hot dog, and the crowd went wild again.

The bleach blond went next, and her biker was much older than the mullet, probably older than Little John, with a vest that said *Los Diablos.* She got bites on the first two tries, but not enough to do more than nick the hot dog. The Diablo wasn't happy about it, but he was fine when one of the other Diablos handed him a full bottle of tequila back in the crowd. He drank it like water. The blond disappeared behind the stage. Too bad. LeAnn saw the Rats cheering in the crowd; she made sure to smile.

That left just LeAnn and the leggy redhead. The emcee replaced the hot dog with a fresh one—"Health code!" he joked—and tossed the half-gnawed one onto the crowd. He chose the redhead over her. It irked her to stand in front of all those people for so long with nothing to show for it. She wasn't an exhibit at the zoo. But she tried to keep her smile on and her shoulders pushed back. The redhead got a biker without a shirt, and on her second try, she bit off nearly half that hot dog with her perfect teeth. Well, not perfect, she had that gap like Madonna. The redhead chewed that hot dog with her mouth open and swallowed. In the crowd, the Dead Rats roared, and Crystal Pete shook a beer over their heads and cracked it open, spraying everyone. LeAnn's neck prickled. This bitch. To more screams, the redhead took off her little macramé bikini top and shook her tits. They weren't even nice tits. Not nearly as nice as LeAnn's boobs. LeAnn imagined pressing the redhead's face against the Harley's hot tailpipe. She snickered when the redhead missed her last chance by a mile, the nubby hot dog getting mustard in her eye. Someone in the crowd yelled, "Chode!," and LeAnn couldn't help but giggle.

This was it: LeAnn's turn. Fucking finally. Maybe this wouldn't be a waste of time. She wiggled her hips and smiled at the crowd as the emcee called for the crowd to produce a biker. They jostled and yelled some more, pushing against one another until finally the mob spit Manuel out. He looked like he was blushing, but he might've been drunk, too. She got behind him on the bike and pressed her boobs against his shoulder blades. She could hear his heartbeat. "I'm going to win," she said. He shrugged under her arms and gunned the bike. She pushed herself up on his shoulders and angled for that dangling hot dog. It hit her in the forehead with a wet slap. She heard them laughing, snorting like pigs. She wiped the mustard off her face and made a point of sucking it off her fingers. A Satan's Brother wagged his tongue at her, and she flipped him the bird. That really made them go wild.

She tapped Manuel's shoulder for the second run. This time, she waited to hoist herself up, waiting until the bike was right under that motherfucking hot dog, and then she shot up. She nearly choked: Two-thirds of the dog made it past her teeth before the rest of it ripped off the hook. She coughed the dog into her hands. It was still intact, save for the mangled end. She raised it over her head to applause. The howls drowned out the emcee, but LeAnn knew what he was saying. She was the best. She won a $1,000. She was the Deep Throat Queen.

In the furor afterwards, she tried to ask the emcee how she could get her money, but he just told her to check with her club. She tried to follow him out of the clearing, but a Dead Rat she didn't know scooped her up from behind and carried her away from the spotlights. There were other men she didn't know, but she could see Ham, Crystal Pete, and Manuel there. The man carrying her swung her up on a stool. Crystal Pete kept shaking beers and blasting them over everyone's heads. Everyone laughing, having a good time. A stereo blasted rock music but the tune was muted under the men's voices. A man with a scraggly beard kissed her neck, and she laughed, pushing him off. She took a beer from one of the raised fists and drank it right down. "Where's my money?" she said.

A couple of the men crowed. "I got your money right here!" one said.

The redhead was probably washing mustard out of her hair at a hand pump.

Someone poured tequila down her shirt, only getting a little in her mouth. The back of her eyes were hot, which she knew meant she was either drunk or sick, and she was betting on the former. Little John probably had her money; he wouldn't lose it. He'd keep it safe for her. A $1,000. She was just having fun.

A big man tugged at her top. She pulled away and tried to put on her best smile, but only half her face wanted to cooperate. Opting for a smirk, she closed her eyes and nestled into the big man's arms. Another hand pushed her top down again, pulling out one of her boobs, then the other. It was cold, but the hands were hot and some were wet. They thumped and slapped and pulled at her boobs. They were laughing, and everyone was just having a good time. Everyone was just being friendly. They knew she was beautiful, and they knew she'd won a $1,000 for being the Deep Throat Queen. She always got hers, she wanted to tell them. Always. She opened her eyes for a second and saw all their wide, grinning faces, eyes shining with drink and adoring. Someone slipped off her shorts and the hands moved between her legs.

Dirt and rocks ground into the small of her back. How she'd ended up on the ground, she didn't know. Her face and hair were wet with something, and everything smelled like beer and sweat. Faces and bodies swam around her, pressed on her, pushed her, pushed into her. They were chanting for the Deep Throat Queen now. They were chanting for her.

SPARROWS

Mike Shaw's mother was the only person waiting for him when the prison guards slid open the heavy, razor wire gate. She sat in her car, the engine running, air conditioner on blast. As he slid into the passenger seat, he noticed how deep the lines around her mouth had become. Her hair, graying at the temples, was pulled taut in a bun at the base of her neck, and he supposed that might be what made her look so old.

"Hey, Ma," he said. He leaned over and kissed her cheek; she smelled of talcum powder. "It's good to see you."

"You smell like cigarettes," she said. The car lighter popped, and she pressed it against the tip of an extra-long menthol Capri. "I set you up in Jesco's old place. Lord knows he don't need it no more."

"What happened to Jesco?" he asked. He fumbled with his front pocket, disappointed to find that his soft pack was crushed. "Can I bum a smoke?"

His mother handed him her pack. "You didn't hear?" she snorted. "I reckon you wouldn't. Last winter he got into it with some ol' boy on the road, and the bastard shot 'im. Shot 'im right in the face."

"What'd they do to the other guy?" Jesco had been Mike's favorite cousin, but they grew apart after Mike's first kid was born and then he got sent up.

"Almost gave the motherfucker a medal. Nobody cares about some dead Shaw." Mike nodded because it was true; his father and uncles were all hell-raisers, fiercely loyal to their name and the women who stood by them. He thought of his ex-wife, Dana, her sandy skin and the wide bridge of her nose. Her face was fuzzy in his mind.

Custer County was nearly 200 miles from the penitentiary, and for the most part, they rode in silence. Mike flipped between radio stations until his mother slapped his hand from the dial.

"Make up your mind! You've been out an hour, and you're already driving me crazy," she said.

He left it on a country station. It was a song he didn't recognize, but he didn't recognize any of the songs. The prairie alongside the highway was as he remembered it save for the white wind towers that loomed over the horizon. At more than thirty stories high, the towers dwarfed the landscape, their heavy arms turning slowly. They looked like pinwheels. Or grave markers.

"How do they keep the birds from flying into them things?" he said.

"They don't."

It was noon by the time they pulled up the gravel drive. The trailer was between two hills, well out of view of the road— Jesco probably liked that. The lot was three acres, fenced, and bordered on all sides by thick woods. An aluminum chicken coop was built into the carport.

"It's about empty, but I got the power on, some propane in the tank. There's a TV—rabbit ears—landline, a few dishes, that old recliner," his mother said. She nodded toward the carport. "Your truck's in there. It drove here, rattled like a sumbitch, but it's got gas. That should set you up." She relit a stubbed cigarette. "Why you looking at me like that?"

"Nothing, Ma," he said. She had a streak of gray in her hair that wasn't there before. "Thanks."

The sun set hours ago, but the thermostat still teetered around one hundred degrees. Patrons of The Office circulated from one side of the bar to the other, hoping to catch a breeze. The bartender, a brunette, opened all the doors and windows, going so far as to set up an industrial fan, but the heat still bore down, worsened by tall glasses of cheap whiskey. Mike was on his sixth. He spun his barstool and tracked the faces in the bar: He recognized some, but in just two weeks he'd learned that most of his old friends had moved on, died, or disappeared. Which were all kind of the same thing, when you thought about it.

He drained his glass and called for another, tapping his cigarette box against the counter in time to the music. The bartender obliged, pouring the whiskey into the dirty glass inches from his face. The caustic scent hit him, and he inhaled it like ether.

"You actually like the taste of this stuff?" The bartender grinned, baring a badly chipped front tooth. A caesarean scar peeked from under her lacy tank top. Mike wobbled his head from side to side.

"Keeps me warm," he said.

She laughed and slapped his arm. "Why haven't I seen you before?" The jukebox whirred as it changed records and a handful of younger men whooped as a Johnny Cash song came on. "You new on the rigs or something?"

"Nah, I just got out."

"Oh, honey," she breathed. "Where'd they have you? My daddy did twenty-five in Stringtown."

"McAlester," he said. He took a cigarette from his pack and lit it. The heat made the smoke waver over their heads. "Yep, ol' Big Mac. Commissary there's only ever got menthols. They kinda grew on me."

"How long were you up for?" she asked.

"I got nine, but it could've been worse," he said. Her eyes were practically watering.

"Could've been on the shelf."

"Oh, they got the death row over there, don't they?" He practically saw her heart flutter. He'd seen a few women like her at the prison, the ones who wrote letter after letter and visited every Sunday. He locked his eyes with hers for a few seconds. The young guys hollered for another bucket of Buds. Sighing, she raised her finger to Mike.

"Hold that thought."

He fucked her on the pool table. She was sweet, her name was Genie, and her ChapStick was cherry-flavored. He was right, she was an ex-con enthusiast, and as soon as he got his shirt off, she asked if he had any jailhouse tattoos. He didn't, but she still did her best to reacquaint him with a woman's touch. He finished, thanked her, left a handful of crumpled bills to cover his tab, and drove home.

That first night, he didn't sleep. He sat up for hours, walking from one end of the trailer to the other, popping that garish orange recliner's footrest up and down, clicking through channels on a loop. It was so goddamn quiet. He cranked up the TV's volume, closing his eyes and letting the sheer noise wash over him. His thumb poised on the remote, he clicked through faster now. Frames warbled on the screen only to dip back out: a woman in pancake makeup sobbing over a 1-800 number became a crowd chanting in a language he couldn't understand in a country he'd never heard of to Johnny Carson standing in front of heavy stage curtains to something called

America's Most Wanted to the multicolored test pattern of an off-air station. The colors reflected off the trailer's nicotine-stained walls, the siren song bouncing back at him in the empty room. The bold lines were comforting in their starkness, their stillness. He turned the TV off, and the screen flickered to black, a white dot in the center, like the inside of a pinhole camera. It became his ritual after that, a nightly regimen that he could follow.

If he did sleep, he woke stunned as if he'd been scolded, hot with embarrassment.

Routine calmed Mike's nerves. With routine, there were no surprises. Every hour presented a task, even if that task was sitting in the chair waiting for exhaustion to lead to sleep. During the week, he circled between the home, the garage, and The Office. Some nights he hooked up with the bartender, others he spent drinking and throwing bones with Tommy and his uncles. They got rowdy, the Strike Axe boys, beating on each other and laughing the whole time. It felt good to be around them, blending in together in their gray coveralls. He didn't want to think about Dana, about waiting, but on the other hand, another day was just another day, and on and on.

One Sunday, two months out from his release, his mother muted the television program and cleared her throat. "You gonna see your kids any time soon?"

He went to his mother's on Sundays. Every week she made a huge pot of corn chowder, and for the next few days she would take the leftovers around to her relatives and friends on her visits. On Sunday, however, she and Mike would sit opposite her boxy television set watching *20/20* and eating corn chowder over aluminum dinner trays. She hated it when anyone talked over the television, movies, or even the radio: All conversation had to occur on a commercial break.

Mike set his spoon down on the tray. It left a yellowish smudge across the painted Coca-Cola logo. He wiped his fingers on the cloth napkin on his knee. "Well, yeah, Ma," he said. "I'm trying to set something up."

"Huh," she said. "You know I talk to her, don't you? You can't lie to me."

"I'm not lying," Mike said. "I'm going to call her."

"This is about your last chance, you understand? They're good girls, hear me," his mother said, "don't you make me choose. You planning on stepping up for them?"

"Yeah, I am," he said. On television, an animated kangaroo jumped out of a yogurt cup. It was creepy, the yogurt splashing like that. He reached for her bowl. "You done?"

"Make sure you rinse the bowls in the sink."

He carried the bowls into the kitchen and ran cold tap water over them. A metallic odor washed out of the pipes. He set the rinsed bowls in the dish rack. In the living room, *20/20's* horn-heavy return theme blared out of the television's speakers.

The next week, he called Dana. He'd come home from his mother's angry; he knew she kept in touch with Dana, but he was never able to gauge how close they actually were. He'd sent Dana a letter just before his release, but being outside froze his nerves. If she wanted to call, she would, right? He was giving her space.

Once the divorce papers went through, she stopped answering his letters, instead sending pictures, and then nothing at all. Her lawyer told him she sold the house and filed for sole custody of the kids, though she agreed to stay in the state. In a way, he understood. It had to be hard, what with the new baby and the oldest still in diapers, to get dropped on your ass like that. For the year the DOC kept him in county, she visited with the girls a few times, and he liked that. The older one, Becca, was finally starting to get some hair on her head when a bed opened up in McAlester. It was a long drive; he understood. Did Becca still have his nose?

The phone rang six times before she picked up.

"Hello?"

"Hey," he said. He began to pace, but the phone crackled if he went more than three feet from the receiver, so he narrowed his track. "Hey, Dana, it's Mike."

"This is Becca."

"Hey," he said. "Hey, Becca, sweetheart, it's—it's Dad. I missed you. I can't believe how grown-up you sound. You doing good, everybody doing good?"

"Dad?" her voice lilted. "I'll get Mom."

Muffled voices carried through the receiver. Mike sat on the kitchen counter and pushed up his shirtsleeves. It was so hot. He tried to reconcile the voice he just heard with the picture of the fat, happy baby he tried to remember. Dana used to say that there were moments where she could see what the girls would look like when they grew up in quick flashes, a glance, when age flickered across their faces, though he'd never seen it himself. He wanted a cigarette, or maybe a drink, but his pack was across the room on the coffee table he jerry-rigged from two wheels and a piece of plywood, and the fridge was beyond the phone's reach.

Dana cleared her throat. "Mike? This better not be collect. I don't pay for long distance."

"Nope, not collect," he said. "Did you get my letter? I was wondering if you and the girls would wanna make the trip, maybe get dinner?"

He thought he heard her snort. "Dinner?" she asked. "Well, give me your PO's number, and I'll see what I can do."

"You don't get a PO if you do the whole bid," he said. His voice shook a little; he cleared his throat, and his hands began to shake. "Becca sounds grown. What grade is she in now? Sixth, yeah?"

"Yeah, middle school," Dana answered. He wondered if she was still wearing her hair short or if she still bit her nails to the quick.

"And Mariah, she's what, damn near ten?" Dana didn't respond. "It'd be great to see them. I need some pictures for the new place. I'm staying out at Jesco's place, you know. Real sad what happened to him." His skin prickled as sweat soaked into his shirt. "But I guess you probably heard about that. Mama said you two talk."

"Mike, can I call you back? I've got dinner on, and I'll have to talk to the girls about coming down," she said. She sounded like a violin that'd been strung too tightly. "I'll let you know, okay?"

"Okay, but listen, Tommy Strike Axe got me a gig at his uncle's machine shop, but I'll be home about six. And the new place, it's got a bedroom, and I was thinking I could set it up for them, you know, with shit they like?" He hurried through his words, standing now. "I mean, now that I'm out, I can take them off your hands on the weekends, you know, like—"

"Mike," she said. "This isn't a good time. I'll call you back."

"Okay," he said. "Tell them I love them."

She'd already hung up.

Dana called on a Tuesday, just as he got home from the garage. He had a couple shots at work, and the blare of the phone made his head ring. But she was in town, and she wanted to meet. Trying to hide his excitement, he suggested The Office, then no, Jerry's, the railcar diner on Main. He and Dana'd gone to Jerry's all the time in high school, always in the middle of the night, after hours, downing stolen liquor in plastic cups.

When he made it into town, Main Street was bustling with people hurrying from shop to shop, trying to beat the downtown bank's clocktower. At eight o'clock sharp, the department store, the pharmacy, and the discount stores shuttered their doors; afterwards, Jerry's was a port at the edge of the world. In the parking lot, Mike hesitated. It would be so easy to turn around and drive away, but he gripped the steering wheel, breathing thickly through his teeth, and switched off the ignition. He wished he had gum.

Inside, the diner was just as he remembered. Black and white portraits of forties' movie stars lined the walls—each signed, almost positively in the same hand. Bette Davis' was off-center, revealing the wall's original white paneling. He spotted Dana in a booth near the bathrooms, an empty coffee cup and a half dozen creamers spread out on the table. She was thin, all angles and elbows, and her hair was cut close to the scalp. She lifted her gaze as he approached and smiled. Her cheekbones could cut glass.

"You look good," she said. She stood and took him in a stiff hug. She strummed her chin. "I like the beard. It suits you."

He bent his long frame into the booth and took care to miss the exposed nail jutting out of the cushion. The fan overhead did little to dispel the lingering scent of old fry oil and Pine-Sol.

"You look good, too," he lied. "How have you been?"

She began stacking the creamer cups in a small pyramid—something she'd done as long as he'd known her. The bones in her wrist snaked gracefully beneath her skin.

"That doesn't really cover it, does it?" she said. Smirking, she toppled the little tower. "I've been waiting so long to scream at you. I thought you ruined my life, the girls' lives." She exhaled and spread her palms on the table. "You did, though. Ruin all our lives. It just got so hard, you know?"

He knotted his hands in his lap. A middle-aged waitress stopped just short of their table. Her eyeliner was electric blue. "Just coffee?"

"Yeah, yeah, that's fine," Mike said. To Dana, "I know I fucked up. And I know sorry isn't worth shit, but I'm sorry."

The silence between them crackled. The waitress brought his coffee without a word, as if she knew it was better to keep her mouth shut. Mike was itching for a cigarette, but Jerry's had gone smoke-free while he was inside. Dana refused to look him in the eyes.

"Every form at their school wants your signature. I had to say it again and again and again," Dana said. She didn't cry, but instead crushed one of the creamer cups in her hand. "Mariah worships you." She laughed. "She keeps all your letters in her jewelry box."

"I wanna see them, please," he said. He was aiming for earnestness, but he knew he sounded desperate. "I wanna know what they look like." He reached out for her and tentatively touched her arm. "I know I fucked up. But I can be better. I can. Let me try." The fluorescent light flickered overhead, and he felt it in his chest. He thought of the stack of photographs in the truck's glove box, every picture Dana had ever sent: birthdays, Christmas, the Fourth of July, but also afternoons in the park, nights after long days, emergency rooms where a smiling little girl waved an arm wrapped in a hard, purple cast. It was like flipping through a magazine. "I wanna know if they look like me."

The girls were staying with Dana's sister, and she wanted to be there for breakfast, so they took their own cars to the trailer. Mike drove carefully, only once taking a swig off the bottle he kept beneath the driver's seat—a habit he picked up from his grandpa. In the darkness of his living room, they fell into each other in all the old ways, retracing steps that, a decade ago, were second nature. Pressed against him, her hips cut into his thighs, and Mike fit his fingers between her ribs, like keys on a piano. He held her face in both hands and thumbed the scar that crossed her right temple.

"You're like a little bird," he said. She laid her head against his chin. "I feel like you might blow away."

"Then hold tight," Dana said.

The next weekend, he made the two-hour trip to Perkins, winding through miles of prairie, then the soft, wooded hills of northern Oklahoma. Dana's house was behind a trailer park, in a row of square, concrete duplexes. All but two of the yards were littered with children's toys. A sign at the corner of her street read *Sunny Acres: A HUD Community*.

When he pulled into the driveway, Dana met him at his window. He leaned in for a kiss, and she glanced back at the house. "Not here," she said.

"Can I come in?" he asked. He tugged at the strap of her tank top. "You look good."

She straightened her strap and stepped out of his reach. "We have to take this slow," she said. "One thing at a time. For the girls, you know?"

He lit a cigarette. "Yeah, sure," he said. His hand shook just a little as he took a long drag. "So, how're we doing this?"

"I figured you could take them to lunch, maybe a movie?" Dana suggested. Her cotton shorts were riding up.

"I'm a mechanic, not a millionaire. They're just inside? I don't have to stay," Mike said. Dana's face remained blank. "I got enough cash to take 'em to McDonald's, but I kinda thought we could just hang out." He gestured toward her house. Out of the corner of his eye, he thought he saw a curtain drop. "You know, like a family?"

"They don't really know you yet," Dana said. She ran her hand through her hair. "I don't think that's a good idea." She turned toward the house and whistled a high, shrill note. Out of habit, Mike's hands shot behind his head. Dana looked at him funny. "What're you doing?"

"Nothing," he said, propping one arm on the window. "You whistle for them like that?"

Before she could answer, Becca and Mariah emerged from the house, the older girl wearing a deep frown. Mike's chest tightened as the two girls stood beside their mother. Mariah had thick, red hair, a trait a couple of his cousins inherited, but she had Dana's eyes, and his mother's wide forehead. Her white T-shirt had a glittery rainbow splashed on its front, but it did little to hide the rounded buds of her breasts. She had a silly stupid grin on her face, and she carried a small, pink purse over her shoulder.

"I'm ready, Mom," she said to Dana. "You can go now."

"Mariah, shut up," Becca said. "You're so *rude—*"

"Come on, not in front of your father," Dana interjected. "There's plenty of time for him to see you fight later. Mariah, get in the truck. You can sit in the middle." Mariah ran to the passenger side, eager to claim her prize.

"You hungry, Becks?" Mike asked. The nickname sounded clunky out of his mouth. No one probably even called her that. The girl rolled her eyes, but she was still beautiful. She had Dana's sandy skin, with his nose and long face, though on her it was almost elegant. If he saw her on the street, he would think her much older than twelve. Already, she stood two inches taller than Dana. He thought about telling her he spent ten years inside a Big Mac but she probably wouldn't think it was a very good joke.

"Sure," Becca said. "I could eat." She hugged Dana and kissed her cheek. "Love you, Mom. Be back soon."

Becca went around the truck and climbed in. Dana held her arms and smiled at him. "They're not too bad," she said. "You'll be alright."

Dana waved until they hit the corner, then disappeared into the house. Mike watched her shrink in the rearview mirror. Sitting so close to the girls, near enough to hear the wheeze that caught in Mariah's throat with every breath, Mike's nerves bristled. His mind cycled through all of the things he thought he ought to say. He had no plan, not anymore. The plan had been to hang out at their house, feel them out with Dana there, maybe spend some time in their mother's bedroom once they'd gone to bed.

"The McDonald's is off the highway. Take this left," Becca said.

"Thanks," he said. Mariah grinned at him from the middle seat. "So, you guys like school?"

"Yes," Mariah said quickly. She looked like a bubble about to burst.

"No, you don't. You fake sick every day," Becca said. "She's just saying that."

"I didn't like school much either," he said.

Up ahead, on the side of the road, two turkey buzzards hulked over a dead coyote. The birds startled as the truck rumbled past, unfurling their impressive wings as they took to the sky.

"You know how you can tell a turkey buzzard from a hawk?" Mike asked.

"One has a nasty face and eats dead stuff," Becca said.

"No, I mean when they're flying," Mike said without missing a beat. "It's their wings, the tips of a turkey buzzard's wings, with those big feathers. From way down here, they look like fingers."

Once they got inside the McDonald's, Mike made an effort to look more relaxed than he felt. Mariah chattered away and giddily told him all about her toys and her friends while Becca looked at him, searching his face for something. The kid behind the counter called out their number, and Mike brought the tray over. Immediately, Mariah dug into her burger, stopping midsentence to take huge, cheek-splitting bites. Becca dipped a french fry in a cup of ketchup.

"She eats when she's nervous," Becca said as she took a bite of her french fry. "You're probably lucky you didn't decide to take us to a buffet. She'll eat herself sick if you let her."

Mariah tried to protest, but her mouth was too full. Bits of chewed burger and processed cheese fell out of her mouth. Mike could smell it, and he tried to keep his face expressionless as he mopped the mess into a napkin.

"So, like, what did you do? Mom won't say," Becca said. Her voice was flat, an affectation he and Dana had often used against each other until it became a joke, an increasingly absurd game. "Did you kill someone?"

Reflexively, he glanced around to see if anyone had heard. No one turned or stared. He met her eyes and, deadpan, said, "I'd probably have gotten less time if I killed someone." A hint of fear flickered across her face, and he tried to smile. "I'm only kidding. It wasn't anything like that." It wasn't, really. Possession of marijuana, second and subsequent. He'd missed a few court dates, too. And his priors. The county always had it out for his people. His mouth was dry, and he sipped at his Coke. "Your mom probably has her reasons. I shouldn't be telling you guys war stories."

"But you were in jail," Mariah said. He could see why she adored him; she wasn't very bright.

"He was, duh," Becca said. She smashed a burnt french fry against the plastic tray. It crumbled. "Grandma said you could be smart if you wanted to."

"Couldn't we all be nice if we wanted to?" he said. He caught something as it passed over Becca's face, but she kept her lips even. "So what else does Grandma say? Anything I should know?"

"She said if Grandpa were alive, he'd kick your ass," Mariah said. She smiled, clearly pleased with herself.

He made it up there every other Saturday for a few months. The boys at the garage understood. Tommy had a kid he didn't see in Owasso. He had his cousin and Mike switch shifts, told him to keep it up as long as he needed. He didn't need more than just the day, it turned out, as Dana made it clear on his second trip that this was about the girls, and only about the girls. He usually made it home by eight o'clock. A proper curfew, he thought.

On the Saturdays Mike didn't leave the county, he drank for free at The Office, waiting until closing for Genie to lock up. She wasn't nearly as pretty as Dana, but she let him sleep in her bed. He found out she was younger than he'd thought: twenty-six, a decade his junior. When they were together, getting stoned on her futon, she talked, an almost constant stream of somethings and nothings. He could sit next to her without a thought in his head while she went on. She had a kid, like he'd guessed, but her mother had custody of it. She didn't say if it was a boy or girl, and there were no pictures in her apartment to tell him any different.

They were lying together like that when Genie sat up and said, "I think you're being too nice to her."

"Who?" Mike hadn't been paying attention.

"Dana," she said. She patted her thigh with her fist. "You did your time. Not like you up and left them. It wasn't your fault." She took his hands in hers. "You're a good man, Mike Shaw."

It was nice to hear her talk like that about him, but the earnest look on her face took him back to The Office the night they met, her with that glassy shine in her eyes as she talked about her dad's stint in Stringtown. His stomach turned. She let his hands drop.

"I can't wait to meet your girls," she said. "Especially the little one. She's so cute in the pictures you showed me."

"She's a lot bigger now," he said.

"Oh, I know, but you know," she said, "I'm just saying. Maybe we'll take them to the zoo in the city. Wouldn't that be fun?" He let her talk, but he knew he'd never follow through on this particular promise.

Dana didn't want him, but Genie would never meet his daughters. Becca had been warming up to him lately, but he knew she'd take the first opportunity to make Genie cry. She was whip smart with an eye for people's weak spots, and Genie was one big walking weak spot.

On his way home from the shop one day, just as the sun was beginning to set, a black cloud rose up from the horizon. It looked like a great, black wall cloud, but it coiled around itself far too quickly. As he got closer, the cloud dimmed, and he saw that it wasn't a cloud at all, but thousands of sparrows, moving not quite in sync, swooping as one into what must have been a swarm of locusts. In all his life, he'd never before seen such a thing. From the south, as if out of nowhere, a hawk dove into the sea of sparrows, breaking their wave as one, then another, dropped out of the sky. The hawk dove again, knocking another sparrow out of the formation, but failing to snag it in its claws.

The third sparrow slapped the pavement just ahead of the truck, and the hawk plunged down, plucking the dead sparrow from the road. Overhead, the rest of the flock scattered, leaving the wide country sky empty.

Most Saturdays, he took them to the Cineplex for matinee showings, when the tickets were cheap. They'd hit up the Dollar Store first, and he'd let them pick three dollars' worth of snacks each, which they were responsible for smuggling in however they thought best. It became a game of sorts, seeing who could fit the most Mike & Ike's in their pockets. One time, Mariah decided that the box itself was unnecessary, and she poured a box of Mike & Ike's into her jacket. The candies tasted vaguely of pocket dust and sand, but she did win that week.

After a midday showing of some kids' movie, he led them out into the bright afternoon sun and asked them how they liked it. He'd found it hard to follow. His eyes were too focused on the sleek shine of the computer animation. Each character looked like they were made of molded plastic; he couldn't read their faces.

"I liked the caterpillar," Mariah said. Her mouth was stained red and blue from the candy. "And the roly-polies."

"Oh, yeah?" Mike said. "I guess they were alright. How about you, Becks?"

Becca thought for a moment, snapping the gum she accumulated from four suckers during the movie. "I guess I liked the ladybug and the spider more this time. And Flick. He wasn't stupid; he just didn't know what he was doing."

"The spider was a little weird," Mike said. He stopped. "What do you mean, 'this time?'"

Becca looked over her shoulder. She shrugged. "I dunno. Mom took us to see it last week," she said. Mike's face grew hot. "I still liked it, though. I wanted to see it again."

He started walking again, toward the truck. He left Becca and Mariah a few steps behind. "What's the point of going to the movies if you've seen it before?" He threw open the passenger door of his truck and waved for them to get in. "Could've thrown my money in the trash."

In the truck, Becca sat in the middle. Her legs were too long for the space, and she leaned toward the passenger side to keep her legs out of the gears' way. "Sorry," she said.

Mike threw the truck into reverse.

Later that night, sitting in his trailer, Mike downed beer after beer in front of his television set. The phone rang, but he didn't get it. It was either Genie or his mother or Dana, and he didn't want to talk to any of them. They all needed so much. His nerves felt raw and, with each ring of the phone, his body tensed. Like a dog backed into a corner, he bristled. He grimaced as he recalled the afternoon. His money wasted; Becca wounded. He took another drink.

He turned the volume on his television all the way up. It was a rerun of *Saturday Night Live*, one of the really old episodes, the one where John Belushi plays a samurai in a deli shop. Every shout from the television reverberated in his head. The laugh track warbled on, though maybe they were real people, maybe not. Who could tell?

REVOLUTIONS

The summer I turned nine was the year my mother decided that I could be trusted to handle myself in public. In truth, she had let me run the empty streets of our neighborhood since I started school, but in public she always made a show of keeping her hands on my narrow shoulders, steering me like a buggy through the grocery store. I had already explored the swampy frog pond that separated our part of town from the country, the abandoned mill with its rusty, hollow silos, and the old chicken hut across the railroad tracks. If she knew where I'd been, she didn't ask, though she asked me a few times to try and keep my knees clean.

When the Free Fair & Carnival came around in early August, I was anxious to try out my new freedom. The fair wasn't free like its name suggested, and it was no powwow, but the lights and the rides and games would run all weekend long. Every year my mother would herd me from kiddie ride to kiddie ride while she gossiped with one of her friends, whistling through her teeth if she thought I'd wandered too far off. The kiddie rides were always a disappointment: a half-painted spinning bear whose red and white suspenders were pink and cream from the sun, a clacking train ride that boasted a five-foot peak and had a penchant for getting stuck at the top, and a swing ride, which I never rode after that time in first grade when Violet Shangreaux forgot to latch the crotch buckle and slid right out of the swing just as the machine hit full velocity. She only broke an ankle and her left wrist, but that was enough to scare me off the swing ride for good.

That year, I had a growth spurt and was finally tall enough to ride the Green Machine, the only ride that wasn't torn down and stored away over the winter. It ran on a converted John Deere tractor engine, and it had two egg-shaped capsules at the ends of welded steel arms that swung up and around like I imagined David's slingshot from the Bible story. It was exhilarating to watch: Some pimple-faced farm boy would kick the motor on, and the dusty black belts would rumble and begin to whir so fast as to appear still before the arms began to swing. Shaniece, my best friend when she happened to be staying with her grandmother (which was often), already made me pinky promise that we would ride the Machine together.

We went to the fair on the second night, a Saturday. I asked my mother's boyfriend, who I called Uncle Pablo, to tie my hair up in a tight bun on the top of my head, and he used one of his red bandanas to hold my hair back from my forehead. In school we learned about the textile factories in faraway New York and Boston and how the people who worked there would get their hair sucked into their machines' gears and pulled out from the root. I imagined the whirring, swinging parts of the Green Machine catching my waist-length hair and taking my scalp with it or worse, more. Uncle Pablo laughed at me when I told him that, but he tied his bandana around my head just the same.

As we walked the quarter mile from our little A-frame in the old part of town, my mother and Uncle Pablo leaning on one another as they went, I ran a few steps ahead. Once we hit those fairgrounds, I'd be home free. I planned how to spend my five dollars' worth of tickets: the Tilt-A-Whirl first, I thought, then the spider ride with its middle painted like a black widow's belly, and then for three tickets, the Green Machine. Or maybe the Ferris wheel instead of the Tilt-A-Whirl, but I knew Shaniece would say that the Ferris wheel was for babies.

My mother whistled for me to slow up as a line of white vans drove past. I stopped and watched, taking a step back into the grassy ditch. There were five of them, mostly identical but for a few differences in year or wear and tear: tall white vans like you see at churches. The orange streetlamp shone dimly through the dark windows, revealing silhouettes of broad-brimmed hats in one van and square bonnets in the next. I was used to seeing the Mennonites around the fair every year, but their presence, all of them dressed so alike, always startled me at first. They weren't like the other white people in Caddo County; they didn't just ignore the rest of us, it was more like they pretended we didn't exist. They kept to themselves on their dairy farms, owned their cows and the land outright, drove their own milk tankers, and seemed to prefer to have as little to do with the rest of us as possible. My mother said that was because of their religion, but Uncle Pablo said it was because they didn't like Indians. Thinking of the girls' milk-white hair caps, how the caps came just over their ears, I touched my own ears sticking out from beneath Uncle Pablo's bandana. My ears felt hot.

As we came up on the fairgrounds lined with Christmas lights—tackiest thing in town, my mother said—I spotted Shaniece sitting on the tailgate of a pickup truck. Even though she was older by ten months (something she liked to remind me of), she was smaller and shorter than I was, and her skin was darker than even Uncle Pablo's. She always wore her thick hair in pigtail-puffs tied with brightly colored hairbands that sometimes had plastic marbles on the ends. We'd known each other since kindergarten, when Shaniece's mother started hustling her down from Oklahoma City whenever school let out, so Shaniece could stay with her grandma. Her grandma lived in the senior housing in the middle of town, and it was never any fun over there. At her mother's house, Shaniece told me, she had cable television and a membership at the science museum. Shaniece was the most sophisticated person I knew. The Free Fair was usually the last big thing we did together every summer because then it was just a week or so until Shaniece's mother would take her home. We prepared for this night by collecting cans from the recycling bin in the Dollar Store parking lot and, when that wasn't enough, we picked up cigarette butts outside the VFW for ten cents apiece.

When Shaniece saw me walking through the dusty lot, she grinned and waved. I got the nod of approval from my mother and jogged to meet her. We slapped palms and stuck our tongues out, a secret handshake we'd already told everyone about. We wasted no time in beelining for the ticket booth. The line was long but moved steadily, and the air was thick with smells; at the far end of the fairgrounds, men stood smoking around the chili and fry bread stands, while others milled around two huge meat smokers that turned out heaping piles of pulled pork. The scent of meat mingled with the smog of cigarettes, sweet cigarillos, and the diesel exhaust that pumped out of more than a few rides. The smell blanketed the grounds, and we would smell it in our clothes for days afterward.

At the ticket counter, the teenage girl behind the register scowled and clicked her tongue as I put down two dollar bills and a small Ziploc of dimes, quarters, and nickels. Shaniece laid down five dollar bills. With a heavy sigh, the girl counted the bills and slid them into her drawer and then counted my coins by scratching them across the counter into small piles. As if it pained her, she ripped ten tickets off the roll and handed them over. "Thank you," Shaniece said. The girl rolled her eyes in a way that made me feel guilty. Shaniece shrugged, so I shrugged, and we joined hands and walked toward the midway where we could cut through the gaming booths to the big rides on the other side. All kinds of people were lined up to play the familiar carnival games: rubber duck race, darts, one of those popgun games, and in a double booth, stacked high with round goldfish bowls, the ring toss, where you could win a sad, three-cent goldfish that would probably die on the way home (Shaniece won four of them one year, and every single one was belly-up by the end of the night). At the end of the midway, fifty or so grannies and grandpas listened with rapt attention to the bingo caller's voice, blue rubber stamps at the ready. Among them I saw Shaniece's grandmother, her silver hair smoothed back in the front and then teased into a white spray.

"Think she'll win anything?" I said, shaking Shaniece's hand in her grandma's direction.

She snorted. "No," she said. "She plays them scratcher cards every day. You wanna do the spider ride first?" She pulled me away from the bingo tent and toward the center of the field.

"Uncle Pablo plays the scratchers sometimes. Once he won twenty dollars," I said.

Shaniece's left eyebrow shot up. "Why do you call him Uncle? He's lived in your house forever. Girl, he's your new daddy, you like it or not."

I sort of nodded and shook my head at once, a mediocre gesture I'd perfected when I was done talking and didn't want to start anything else. But I knew even then that Shaniece was at least half right: Uncle Pablo had been around forever, he was kind, and I liked the way he wore his hair, long and shiny like my grandpa's in all those yellowed pictures we had on our fridge. He was Cheyenne, not Choctaw like us, but not white like my real father. I probably liked that best about him.

To our left, the carousel's generators hummed, nearly drowning out the Classic Country station blaring through the carousel's speakers. The carousel's roof was lined with mirrors cut into puzzle shapes, and the mirrors reflected the flashing lights from the Ferris wheel and the other rides. It was disorienting, like falling into the center of a kaleidoscope, but this only made me giddy. We settled at the end of the line for the spider ride, a half dozen or so Mennonite boys ahead of us. They looked like slightly imperfect copies of one another, all tall and wide-shouldered, with dusty blond hair sneaking from beneath their straw hats. They were most likely brothers, or maybe first cousins. They had the clearest blue eyes I'd ever seen, like the bottom of the public swimming pool. One of the younger ones caught me staring and winked, and a full blush creeped over my chest and face. He smirked and turned back to the other boys as the line moved up. The boys were the last to get on the ride, and they took the steps in near-identical pairs, two by two.

"My grandma says don't talk to the Mennonites," Shaniece said in a whisper.

"I like their eyes," I said. "I don't know nobody with eyes like that." My eyes were dark brown, though not so dark as Shaniece's.

"My grandma says it's because they don't go mixing with us and we should do them the same," she said, "like they can come out here and play nice and all, but they're not having babies with us." I made a face. Sex was still a repulsive but fascinating thing to me; while I understood what it was, the physical act was practically unimaginable. I blew a raspberry, and Shaniece rolled her eyes. "I'm tired of talking about this," she said. "I want to go on the ride already. Damn."

Cussing still held its glamor that year, and we practiced using certain expletives when we were alone. *Shit* and *damn* were our favorites, the hard clip of the former and the sigh of the latter. We tried the word *fuck*, but it always seemed to come out wrong, not at all like how the teenagers in the park said it. This word, we concluded, would come to us later, and then we would understand. For the summer, though, we contented ourselves with brief brushes with maturity by cussing under our breath.

The spider ride started up, its massive axis grinding to life, lifting its eight legs up above the crowd. The little carriages on each leg began to spin independently. The gears groaned in waves, just as the passengers' screams rose and fell. In three of the carriages, the Mennonite boys threw their weight from one side of the car to the other to maximize their spin. The boy who winked at me was smiling, yelling, and holding tight to his hat. The blue of his cotton shirt matched his eyes. I wondered what it would be like to grow up in a world filled with slight versions of yourself; I thought about how my mother's skin was darker than mine, Uncle Pablo's darker than hers, and Shaniece's darker still.

"You're staring," Shaniece said.

I looked at the ground, at the little rips and tears in the grass from the metal barricade around the spider ride.

"Keep dreaming," Shaniece said. "A Mennonite boy's gonna marry a Mennonite girl, and they're gonna have Mennonite babies. That's how it goes. You ever see a Mennonite boy with an Indian or a Black girl? They stick to their own."

"I know," I said. I wondered what my real father looked like. Did he have blue eyes and blond hair? My mother said she met him in college, her second year, and that he was studying to go to vet school. He was very tall, which said something since she wasn't a little thing herself. I wondered if he knew about me. That was something my mother wouldn't tell me. "Do you think they sleep in those hats?"

Shaniece laughed. "Probably."

After we rode the spider ride, we walked on uneasy legs over to the Tilt-A-Whirl. My hip ached from where it had been crushed up against the plastic carriage on every downswing, but I was still high on the feeling of spinning over the lit up fair, the people and lights below melting into a flurry of color and noise.

"That was so fun," I said. "I wish we had enough tickets to ride it again later." I stepped around a puddle of melted ice cream.

"Nah, if we had more tickets, we should ride the gravity spinner. That's the one where it sucks you back to the wall," she said.

"It's called center-pedal force, what sucks you to the wall," I said.

"I knew that. They got a little one at the science museum, and I've been on it tons."

The line to the Tilt-A-Whirl was short, to our surprise, but it soon became apparent why. From the inside of one of the oversized teacups, a rancid odor of whiskey wafted from the plastic seats. Someone had vomited, presumably the teenager curled into a ball on the ride's walkway. The attendant and a few other men were trying to clean the seat and carry him off the plank. They grabbed his shoulders and began to drag him toward the ramp, and he lifted his face and moaned before dry heaving on the grass. I recognized him as one of the Shangreaux boys. The Shangreauxs had the worst luck. I tugged on Shaniece's hand.

"Shit," I said, "I don't wanna ride nobody's puke."

"Me neither," she said. She pointed toward the gravity spinner. "C'mon, then."

We cut across the midway hand in hand, running. There was no urgency, no hurry, but we ran anyway until we were breathless, skidding to a stop in the soft grass. Our shoes left little ruts in the dirt. I felt a line of sweat drip down my cheek. I always felt like I was running with Shaniece, running after her, even when I knew she was feeding me a line or I disagreed with her. Across the fairgrounds, the carousel spun slowly, blasting its warbling music, the slow pump of its horses creeping at a snail's pace.

Shaniece stopped running in front of the gravity spinner. It was one of the bigger rides, and we were quickly at the head of the line. We watched the people in front of us strap themselves into the individual slots before the attendant came by and jerked their belts to check them. They spun for a while, and when the spinner tilted sideways, I saw the floors were painted to look like a roulette wheel. I imagined it spinning off its base like a stripped lug nut, careening out of the fairgrounds and into the town. When the ride was over, the passengers' faces were flushed bright red, all of them, and they seemed happy to have their feet on solid ground once more.

We handed our tickets to the attendant and picked two slots, hurrying to strap in. I squared my feet against the back of the wall, trying in some way to dig my heels into the steel floor. Other riders filled in, picking slots here and there. Last to step onto the floor were the Mennonite boys.

They were laughing and jostling one another as they took up the last remaining spaces. The attendant made his round, checking our belts, and returned to his control box to flick the switches. I squeezed my eyes tight, prepared for the slow whir that would begin the ride. I peeked out of one eye and saw the boy, his hat held with both hands across his chest, his short hair crimped from the crease of his hatband. He looked ready to be buried. I felt a rising in my stomach that before that moment I thought was shame, and it was then, too, but not entirely. I closed my eyes again.

The ride jerked and began to spin clockwise. I groped for Shaniece's hand and squeezed until she squeaked, her fingers twisting between mine. We spun, faster and faster, and I felt my body lose its weight into the wall behind me, a feeling of both weightlessness and absorption. Shaniece screamed a high, happy scream, and I joined in, whooping. When the spinner tilted sideways, we both laughed hysterically, the pressure of the air sucking the breath from our lungs. The other passengers were a blur, my eyes unable to focus on anything but Shaniece's hand in mine and the pinwheeling sky overhead.

As the gravity spinner slowed to a stop, I felt myself sink back to the steel floor. I felt heavier than before, more tethered to the ground. My skin tingled. Shaniece was still giggling, her palm wet and cold in my own. "That," she said, gulping for air, "was awesome." She unsnapped her belt. "That was so much better than the Tilt-A-Whirl."

"Yeah," I said. "Maybe." I unbuckled the canvas straps and followed her to the gate.

"Green Machine," she said.

I nodded. Between the spider ride and the gravity spinner, a line of twenty or so people coiled around the Green Machine. We found a spot in line and watched the people on the Green Machine do loop-de-loops in their cars, screaming in waves. The arms were at their zenith, and a few coins fell loudly to the ground; the crowd laughed. The attendant did it every year. Riders were supposed to empty their pockets before they got on, and inevitably someone wouldn't. "Send down your wallet," someone in line said. I read once that if you dropped a penny from a great enough height, you could kill someone, and I didn't want that on my conscience.

"No pockets," Shaniece said, pointing to her shorts. She tapped the side of her head. "Smart, right?"

"Yeah," I said.

We waited like that through two turns, and with each step closer to the head of the line, I felt a new wash of cold sweat at the base of my neck. The gravity spinner had loosened my bun, and damp strands were stuck to my neck and shoulders. With every revolution of the Green Machine's arms, a gust of air burst out at us, thick with the smell of diesel and dirt. The smell caught in my throat. I jerked on Shaniece's elbow. "I don't think I can."

"What do you mean you can't? We've been waiting forever. We got three tickets left," she said. "You can't chicken out."

"I'm not a chicken," I said. My knees felt like they were filled with helium, ready to lift me off the ground.

The line moved forward and us with it. Her eyebrows were knit together like they were when she was angry. "You are so a chicken. Why did you even come here if you weren't gonna play with me?"

"I don't want to ride this ride," I said. The cars were unloading, and I knew we would be included in the next group. The thought made my heart beat too fast. "I'll share my tickets with you."

Shaniece looked at the Green Machine, with its wheezing belts and pimple-faced attendant, and then looked back at me. "I won't be your friend anymore if you don't do this with me."

"That's not fair," I said.

"Say you're a chicken," she said. "Say it and I'll still be your friend."

"I won't."

"You have to." She wrinkled her nose and stomped her foot.

Behind us, the Mennonite boy came off of the Green Machine. As he passed, his hat still in his hands, Shaniece tugged at his shirt sleeves. "Hey," she said. "You know she likes you. She wants to have sex with you."

A look of confusion crossed the Mennonite boy's face as he glanced from Shaniece to me and then to his friends. They burst out laughing. All of them. My eyes were hot, and I knew that tears were coming. Shaniece, satisfied, skipped around them to the front of the line. I covered my face with my hands, but through my fingers I saw her hand her tickets over and hop into the capsule. The boys were saying things in German, already drifting away from me, slapping each other on the shoulder as they laughed. The Mennonite boy smiled at me as he followed them, which only made me feel worse.

I didn't move as the line snaked around me like water over rocks. I watched as the attendant started flicking switches on the panel. My palms were slick with my tears and a bit of snot that had found its way down my face. I recognized Shaniece's laugh, shrill like a bird's, drifting out of the ride as its arms began to swing. When the arms hit the first peak, a split second before swinging back faster, that laugh became a high whine. Another turn and she was wailing. I looked at the people around me, children and adults, Mennonites and Indians, but no one seemed to hear it. The attendant flipped a different switch, locking the Green Machine's arms high overhead. The wailing stopped. A coin clanged down out of the cage. A Mennonite girl's haircap fell softly in the grass. A cigarette. A few people in line patted their heads, looking at the sky. Rain, I heard one say, but the sky was clear, pocked with stars.

When the Green Machine had run its course, I waited for Shaniece outside the exit gate. She had hurt my feelings, but I had no one else and it didn't sound like she had much fun anyhow. I thought surely she would forgive me and we could split my last tickets for a game or a ride on the Ferris wheel. One by one, everyone else slipped through the gate, but Shaniece did not. I walked around the fence, searching for her. I saw her first, climbing awkwardly over the little metal fence before crouching between two small bushes, her arms straight as planks over the rest of her. The seat of her shorts was shades darker than the rest, a wide, wet spot. She turned and opened her mouth, her eyes angry, but instead of saying anything, her eyebrows wrinkled together.

"Don't tell," she said.

"I won't," I said. "Want I should tell your grandma we're going home?"

"Yes," she said. She stared at the ground. "Did anyone see?"

I shrugged, "Thought it was raining."

"Really?" She smiled at that.

"Yeah."

Shaniece stopped coming to Caddo County after that. Her mother married a businessman, and he was moving them both to California, or that's what Shaniece said. We wrote letters for a while; hers were all postmarked Toledo, Ohio. Her grandmother moved along with them. A white family moved into her yellow house and painted it white even though Uncle Pablo warned them it would be gray in a season.

One of the Mennonite boys died that spring. He fell into a grain silo and suffocated, or drowned. I didn't know if it was the same Mennonite boy from the fair, but it could have been. I was in a high school German class when I finally understood what those boys had said. *Nein danke.*

I hadn't known it then, but that was my last Free Fair, too. I never got to ride the Green Machine. A recession was setting in and everyone was scrambling for work. Uncle Pablo got hired at a spring factory in Tulsa, so we packed up and moved along with everyone else. Our new house was a duplex in a block of newer developments. From the roof, you could see the lights of downtown, glittering in hot whites, pale yellows, and golds. As the nights went on, the skyscrapers' windows would flicker out, one by one, until only a few remained, floating, unmoored against the night sky.

SHELLS I

Tommy wasn't ready to go home. It had been six days since Donna and the baby were discharged from the hospital, and the house seemed to close up around them. For nearly a week, he woke with the sun and told Donna, doped up and perpetually naked, that he was going to look for a job. He didn't tell her that there were no jobs, or that he spent the past four days with his uncles at The Office, a roadhouse off SH-54.

Now, a little drunk and dizzy from the heat, Tommy hooked a left at the creek and headed north to Dead Woman's Curve. The narrow strip of road weaved dangerously around the hills, earning Dead Woman's Curve the secondary title of Dead Indian Curve, but Tommy could field the bends with his eyes closed. He'd spent a good number of years drag racing up and down the two-mile stretch; back then he had a '71 Camaro, but he lost it to some townie from El Reno.

The truck rumbled over the bridge, and the asphalt turned to gravel. Tommy pulled off into the ditch and popped the glove box, rummaging around for the tin of pot he kept there. There wasn't much left, but he rolled a pinner anyway, throwing open the door and starting down the dirt path to the creek. It was June, and the Oklahoma sun bore down on him with increasing intensity. His dark hair, tied back in a loose braid, burned against his scalp.

Busted cement littered the creek bed, rebar twisting out at odd angles, leftovers from when the county decided to widen the bridge. Red silt washed around the blocks, staining their sides the color of rust. Tommy used them like stepping stones, using the rebar to hoist himself across. He settled himself on the largest slab that dug into the creek's middle at the slightest incline, took out the pinner, and struck a match. He lit the joint and took a few drags. Thick plumes of smoke descended from his nostrils as he coughed.

The creek was bordered by a dense tree line, thick with leaves and creeping ivy. The locusts thrummed, their song echoing off the underside of the bridge. A flock of barn swallows had made their mud nests all along the bridge's lip, and the mother birds dove low before returning to their nests.

He dragged on the joint and watched the birds. After watching the swallows for a while, he reasoned it wouldn't be too hard to build a house out of mud. The Pueblos built whole cities from adobe, carving their plots out of the hillside. His own people, the Pawnee, had been here long before the roads and oil rigs, but they were all long gone, pushed northeast past the city. Donna's family was Cheyenne, and he knew she'd never leave Caddo County, even though they were holed up in a two-room throwback to Dust Bowl deserters on an acre of dry, red clay. They were getting by on food stamps and the charity of Donna's parents, who owned the land and the house and who kept the electricity running. When Donna got pregnant, his uncles told him to bail, to grab his shit and run, but he didn't. He stayed.

He stubbed out the joint on the slab and sat up, catching the scent of a dead animal on the wind. Ignoring it, he closed his eyes, but the smell worsened until he found himself eying the banks for its source. Upstream, moving slowly with the rippling current, was the largest turtle Tommy had ever seen. The stench blew off its shell and, from a distance, he guessed it was nearly as wide as his arms were long. Its carapace was dark green and faceted like a prehistoric, geodesic dome. As it drew closer, Tommy scooted to the slab's edge and waited for the turtle's carcass to drift close enough to touch. He wanted to examine his unusual find. When it was within arm's reach, he rocked forward on his heels and tried to get a grip on the shell's edge. It was heavier than expected and when he pulled it from the water, what could only be the turtle's remains poured from the shell as if from a sieve. Bits of rotten flesh splashed into the water. Tommy's stomach heaved; his first instinct was to shove the thing into the water and let it continue on its way. But on the other hand, he wanted it.

"Damn near big enough for a man in there," he muttered between his teeth as he held his breath and, tightening his grip on the shell, shook the last of the turtle into the creek.

Once emptied, he lifted it toward the sun and peered through it. The interior of the shell was flecked with waterlogged meat, and the underside shone with scum. Appraising the path to the truck, he knew he'd have to wade the creek if he wanted to take it home.

By the time he pulled into the drive, he reeked of sweat and decay. He unloaded the shell from the truck and propped it against the house. Leaving it there, he almost skipped to the house, he was so excited. The lights were off when he went inside, and the air was stale. There was an uncapped ketchup bottle on the kitchen floor. Donna's pain pills were on the stove, and Tommy saw that she only had a handful left. The prescription was for thirty, and her mom had filled it for her the day after her caesarean section. He unscrewed the cap and reached for one of the round, blue pills. His fingers left greasy smudges on the inside of the amber bottle, and when he popped the pill into his mouth, it tasted faintly of creek water.

A soft whine came from the bedroom. He stepped across the linoleum and stopped just short of the door. Catching himself in the hall mirror, he laughed. His hair was tangled and wild, his arms and chest smeared with dirt and sweat. He clucked his tongue and quietly pushed open the bedroom door.

"Donna?" He whispered. "Psst, Don?"

Donna lay naked on the bed, her eyes hazy with medication and the baby nestled against her thigh. Her skin was bright against the jaundiced baby's skin. She turned down her face, glimpsing her wound, and tears ran down her face. For the first time since the operation, he looked at her abdomen; he noted the intricacies of the purple and yellow bruises that blossomed from her middle onto her wide hips like a child's watercolor. The surgeon told him that they used 200 staples to close her up. Tommy had thought her pregnant belly was beautiful, the way it swelled outwards from her long frame and how she could balance a bowl of popcorn on its crest when they watched late-night broadcasts of *Dynasty*. He stood in the doorway a moment before moving to sit on the bed's edge.

"Hey," she whimpered. The baby kicked in its sleep.

"Hey," he said. He ran his gaze up and down her body and recalled the names he gave the freckles on her thighs— names like Emmett and Petunia, but he couldn't remember which was which. "You alright?"

"It hurts so much, Tommy," she said. "I didn't think it could hurt this much."

"You need me to get your pills?" Tommy asked hesitantly.

"I already took some, and it still hurts," she said. A sob escaped her throat. "And it's ugly."

"The baby?"

"No, this." She waved her hand angrily at her stomach. She covered her face with her hand. "This isn't what it was supposed to be like."

He caught himself mapping her stretch marks with his forefinger. Withdrawing his hand, he searched for something beautiful about the jagged gash that ran from navel to pubic bone. His mouth began to water, and his esophagus tightened. He looked away. "Come on, Don, I gotta surprise for you," Tommy offered. She uncovered one eye and sniffled.

"Really?" There was a pause. "What's that smell?"

"Not really part of your surprise, but more of a necessary evil," Tommy said. He stood up and offered her his hands.

She shook her head. "You stink, Tommy, you should shower before you do anything else," she said.

"Come on, it's really neat, it'll only take a sec," he said. He got up and motioned for her to follow.

"Look at me." She stayed prone on the bed. "Whatever it is, you're gonna have to show me from here."

"It's outside," he said. "I think you'll get a real kick out of it."

She curled an arm protectively around the baby. Her dilated eyes narrowed.

"How'd your job hunt go?" she asked.

"Same as it has for the past year," he said. "Now come outside, I brought you something."

"Are you even trying, Tommy?" She began to cry again.

"You know, there was a time when a man would bring something home for his wife and she wouldn't give'im any shit, hell, she'd be happy," he said. He paced the bedroom, suddenly angry.

"This isn't that kind of time."

"Damn right, it's not. Instead, I got you bitching at me, sitting there like a gutted fish." His voice rose, and the baby stirred next to her. She sobbed.

The pill began to kick in, and the air around him went fuzzy. His body felt tired, and guilt washed over him with the pill's warmth. It occurred to him that Donna must feel this way, too. He turned and left her and the baby there.

Outside, flies had made a home in the shell. He took off his shirt and used it to swat away the flies. Even without his shirt, he could still smell himself, so he stripped down to his underwear. There wasn't a neighbor for miles, and if someone made it their business to drive all the way out here, then that was their own fault. He laid his shirt, pants, and socks on the hood of the truck, looping his boot laces over the ram's head hood ornament. The burnt summer grass crunched beneath the soles of his feet. He bent low and examined the shell closely, tracing its contours with open palms. He fingered the thin bones that held the top to the bottom and, hooking one foot with the bottom half, he tugged upwards. The bones cracked loudly.

His toes slipped on the slimy interior, and his foot slid into the shell. The protruding vertebrae scraped against his heel. Wiggling his foot free, he tried again and managed to crack the halves at their bridge. He laid the two pieces side by side.

"You musta been one old son of a bitch, huh?" he said.

The wind rocked the shell's top. It was about half the size of those turtle-shaped kiddie pools and twice as deep.

Tommy stepped inside it carefully and crouched down, bringing his knees to his chest.

"Imagine living your entire life," he said, "then you die, and some dick desecrates your body." Something squelched between his toes, and he stood up.

He dragged the top half to the water spigot and turned it on full blast. The water pressure worked at the remaining bits of flesh as he scrubbed at them with his bare hands. Waterlogged and rotten, it was like scraping Jell-O out of a bowl. It wasn't difficult work, and once he washed away the meat and its accompanying slime, the shell's interior was actually smooth and gold, like tiger's-eye. The bottom was a different story: Strings of muscle and sinew clung tight to the bone. He scraped at it until the tips of his fingers were raw. Satisfied that the shell was as clean as he could manage, he set them back up against the house. The sun had already gone down, and though he ducked his head under the spigot's stream, he didn't mind the smell. It had grown on him in the evening hours.

He leaned against the truck's grill and examined his work. The shell didn't resemble itself like that, dismembered and laid up. Tommy tried to count the rings, the years this cavern had seen. When he was a kid, his uncles told him you could guess a turtle's age by counting its rings, or maybe that was trees, but he tried, and anyway, his turtle's shell was covered in blunted domes, and the rings were indistinguishable from the knobby bumps that rose out of each dome.

"You're a right dinosaur," he said. "Been round longer than any of us."

As far as he could tell, there'd been no movement in the house after Donna stopped crying. Inside, things were as they had been: The ketchup was on the floor, the pills on the counter. Tommy counted them: three less than before. He saw the breast pump in the sink, leaking the last of its bounty into the drain. He put the ketchup in the refrigerator and took out a beer. The door clicked as he shut it. It was an older model, one that locked from the outside. He took a drink of his beer. A few years back, he'd seen a story on the news about a little boy who went missing a few counties over. Someone found him six months later in a junk pile a quarter mile from his house, dead inside an old fridge.

He downed the beer and went to the bedroom. Donna lay curled in a ball at the far corner of the bed, her face burrowed against the wall. She slept under a short afghan, her bare toes on pointe. Beneath the blanket, he could see she hadn't dressed. Her arms circled her stapled stomach.

The crib was quiet at the bedside. Before the baby was born, Donna's friends went on and on about how little sleep they'd get, but he hadn't heard the baby cry since the hospital. Gently, Tommy reached into the crib and picked the baby up. Its head fit easily in his palm, and its feet barely touched the crook of his elbow. At the hospital, Tommy had held the baby at arm's length, but in the bedroom, he held it close like he'd seen Donna do when she breastfed. The baby was dark, but had a shock of fine, dark hair on its crown, a few strands of white at its nape. The doctor said the white would grow out. The baby jerked in its sleep, smacking its waxy lips.

"You already know it's no use crying around here, huh?" Tommy whispered.

He lay down with the baby on his chest. He could feel its hot breath. Suddenly he swooned for the baby, his baby, and thought about reaching out to Donna, waking her, but he couldn't bring himself to touch her. Her body was familiar, but she was as unrecognizable as his shell. As he began to fall asleep, he moved the baby beside him and draped his arm around its tiny form.

He woke in the middle of the night to what he was sure was the sound of steam coming off Donna's piss. From a sound sleep he heard it: The pressurized stream against the porcelain bowl, the slow hiss that made him open his eyes in the dark, wide awake. The walls thinned, and he heard her padding down the hall to the kitchen—she ran her hand along the wall, her fingernails dragging along uncovered drywall—the pill bottle rattled, the faucet ran. When Donna crawled back into bed, she tried to curl herself around him. He pulled the baby closer and scooted away from her, pretending to be asleep.

When the sun started its ascent, he woke again. Mud had flaked off his back and legs in the night, and it itched. He was aware of the raw odor that came off him in waves. Beside him, the baby yawned and slept on. Its chest rose and fell ever so slightly with each shallow breath. He clutched the baby and got up. Donna, deep in a codone slumber, he imagined, slept on. He hadn't diapered the baby before he fell asleep, and the baby had wet the bed.

Taking the baby to the kitchen, he wet a washcloth and wiped it down. The baby's limbs were loose, and he raised each hand twice before letting it fall. It hardly stirred as he put on its diaper. Tommy grabbed a sheet from the closet and swaddled the baby.

"You're safe with me," he said.

Taking the baby in his arms, he ducked outside. The storm door's screen popped out of its aluminum frame as it swung shut, but he ignored it. He smiled when he saw his shell, dry and free of the mess that had been at its center the day before.

"This is for you, little one," Tommy said. He set the swaddled bundle in dewy grass, within sight of the shell. "Your own little shell to keep you safe. Just a few more touches and it's yours."

Sitting on his knees, he took the top half of the shell in his arms and ran his fingers over its surface. Cleaned of algae and creek scum, the top was still dark green, brown veins circling each ridge. He replaced it and stood, wiping his hands on his underwear. Mud and yellowed sweat streaked the band. He hopped from one foot to the other in an effort to take them off, but he slipped, and his bare ass hit the ground with a slap. Without getting up, he glanced at the baby. Its eyes were fixed straight up at the sky.

He pushed himself up, not bothering to brush off the dirt, and retrieved a hammer and nail from the toolbox in his truck. He returned to the top half of the shell and made a mental x on the thickest section of the bridge that held the shell together. Holding the nail steady, he brought the hammer down and felt the bone give a little. He brought the hammer down again and again, the third swing falling foul and busting open his knuckle. Not thinking, he wiped the back of his bloody hand across his face, tasting blood, sweat, and dirt. He could feel his heartbeat in the nerves of his hand as he pushed the nail through. He repeated the process with the bottom half, rocking back and forth on his heels.

"One more thing," he said. The baby was still awake, and Tommy was surprised by how blue its eyes still were. The doctor said the baby would grow out of that, too.

He rolled the shell onto its top and lifted the bottom half to it. The two holes lined up, almost perfectly. He rummaged through his toolbox until he found some baling wire; he snatched it and quickly broke off a good-sized piece. He was beginning to feel the same excitement he felt when he found the shell. Giddy, he worked fast at winding the wire through the holes, tightening his loops. He bent the twisted end around the outside of the shell: He didn't want the sharp points on the inside.

Reunited, the shell had large gaps where its former tenant had extended its limbs. Tommy tested his hinge: The bottom half of the shell swung open and closed.

"See? I'm good for something, huh?" Tommy picked up the baby, holding it over the reconstructed shell. Holding the baby with one hand, he stroked the shell's underbelly. The sky already shimmered with heat, and Tommy welcomed the warm morning wind that washed over them. The baby's fists fought against its cotton wrap; it was the most he'd ever seen the baby do, and it delighted him.

"Tommy?"

Donna sounded as if she were at the end of a tunnel. She called for him again, but he didn't want to answer.

"Shh," he said. He rocked the baby gently. "It's alright."

He lifted the shell's lid and delicately lowered the baby into it. He made sure the baby rested to the side of the bony spine and that the sheet was tucked tight around its head. He touched the baby's lips.

"Tommy?" He heard her footsteps in the hall. "Do you have the baby?"

The baby trained both blue eyes on him and stuck its tongue out.

JOYRIDE

I'm behind the wheel of my dad's 1987 Bronco. It's his weekend, and he decided that it's time I learn to drive. I am eight years old, and it's the middle of the night, and the rain comes down in hard, heavy sheets. He's drunk like he is on most of our weekends, a secret I keep from Mom because for four days a month he is there with me and me with him. He is slumped in the passenger seat, his breath coming in quick bursts and, in the glare of the porch lamp, his face shines. He is a tall man, and his knees are pressed hard into the dashboard as he tries to move the seat back; it's stuck, and he kicks the floorboard.

"Well, c'mon now, AJ," he says. "Turn 'er over."

I sit on the edge of the seat, holding the steering wheel tight so I can see. I am tall for my age, taller than any of the boys in my class, but not that tall, and he hasn't pushed the seat forward for me. His heavy fists rest in his lap, fingers curled around the glass neck of a bottle of Burnett's Flavored Vodka. He lost the cap somewhere between the house and car, and now the car smells like peppermints and nail polish.

He raises his free hand in the dark, and I turn the ignition like I've seen him do. I hold it for a second too long, and the engine screeches angrily. My hands are shaking as I scoot off the seat.

"Hold your foot on the brake," he says. He reaches between us and tugs the gear shift down three notches. "Let up now."

I do, and the car rolls forward. "Shit, fuck, brake," he says. I jam my foot on the brake again as the Bronco's cattle guard butts up against the gray lattice that lines the porch. He grunts and slams the gear up one notch. I feel us settle into reverse. "Lights and wipers."

"Huh?"

"Turn on the lights and wipers. You wanna get us killed?"

So many knobs and switches. I pull the biggest one first because it has a headlight drawn on it, and the lights flash on. Another knob dims the dash light, a button turns on the flashers. "Dad?" I need him to show me, but he just runs his thumb around the rim of his bottle. I'm afraid of hitting the wrong button again, but I feel along the turn signal until I find the knob at the end. I turn it until the wipers swipe frantically across the cracked windshield. I'm relieved. "Now?"

"That's my girl," he says. His head sort of wobbles as he turns to look out the rear windshield. "You're clear. Bring her back slow."

I do. He slaps me on the shoulder; it catches me, and I squeak. "Easy stuff. Now it's automatic, all you gotta do is put it in drive." I can't quite get the gear to move down until I use both hands, and he laughs at that, taking a drink. "Cooking with gas now, huh."

It takes me a few tries with the gas pedal. First too hard, then too soft, stop-starting past his little gray house with the gray lattice. The Bronco's wide tires crunch over the gravel drive at the end of his plot, and I get the car ambling toward the county road. It reminds me of riding the go-karts, the way you jolt at first. I'm glad there's no one around to see us. For as long as I can remember, he's lived out here in the sticks, with the coyotes and the rusted-out oil rigs, and every season the drive washes out until it's just two deep grooves zigzagging down the hill. Mom probably hated it out here.

I am afraid to do anything but look straight ahead, toes extended to press the pedals. The headlights bounce as the Bronco slides into the grooves in the road like marbles on a track. A pair of bright eyes flash in the ditch. I try to get a glimpse of my dad's face. I need him to talk to me. He is a talker, and his quiet makes me doubtful. When he doesn't talk, Mom says you can see the gears working, but I only see his long hair unraveled, a loose smile on his face. His white teeth shine in the dark as he twists the knob on the radio. A country song, a car dealership commercial, a radio preacher: Bits and pieces of sound scramble into one another. He hums something.

"You're doing great, kiddo," he says. "A regular Richard Petty, huh."

"The singer?"

"Nah, the King," he says. He clicks his tongue. "Only the greatest NASCAR driver of all time. Shoot, girl, I thought I raised you better."

"I'm sorry," I say.

"Oh, c'mon," he says. In front of us, the headlights reflect off the T sign at the end of the drive. The sign's dotted with holes from buckshot. "You're gonna wanna stop right here, we're making a left."

I pump the brakes, bringing us to a hard stop. He reaches over me and flips the blinker. "That way." The blinker is loud, adding a ticking rhythm to the static coming through the radio. Faintly, a Spanish song warbles in and out.

"Where're we going?" Beyond the headlights is nothing but darkness, and the faraway flicker of the wind turbines' red safety lights. In the daytime, the turbines look like white stick figure giants standing on the plains, watching, occasionally spinning their arms, but at night they're invisible but for those mean red eyes. My dad calls them sentinels, which Mom said means they keep watch.

"That way," he says. "Getting there's half the fun. Your mama used to say that. C'mon, AJ, just take the turn slow like."

Here at the bottom of the hill, the wind whips around the Bronco, whistling through the frame. The wet asphalt looks slick under the headlights. Cold blooms in my stomach and flowers up to my shoulders. The turbines wink at me. "I'm scared," I say.

"Ain't no fear out there," he says. He takes a drink from his bottle and smacks his lips. "You know Richard Petty got hisself in a bad one on his last ride—his car was on fire and he, what did he do? He climbed out the damn window." He laughs and drinks again. Some of the vodka spills down his chin. "You got nothing to worry about, kiddo. I'll drag you out the window myself. Remember now, no power steering on this old boat, so make sure you turn that wheel."

I take a deep, shaky breath and let off the brake, letting the Bronco roll onto the county road. He's right about the steering. I can feel the car resisting, and I use my weight to pull it out. For a couple seconds my foot isn't even on the pedal. I steer us onto the road, give it a little gas, and he whoops. "I did it," I say.

He bobs his head. "Yeah, yeah, you did," he says. He points. "Take the center lane. These tires were expensive."

"What if somebody comes the other way?"

"You'd see their lights first."

"Even in the rain?" My chest feels cold again.

"You'll see their lights first, AJ."

I do as he says and press the gas until we're riding smooth at thirty miles per hour. It feels faster, like the downswing on the spider ride at the carnival.

The radio whines as he flips it to an oldies station, to a song I recognize off one of his records. "This is a good one," he says. His words melt into one another, and he fumbles in his pockets, probably looking for his smokes. "Ophelia," he sings, "where have you gone, bap, bap, bada-bap." He taps the horn parts out on his knees, and when I look at him, his eyes are closed.

"Should I go faster?" I say. Part of me wants him to say yes, yes, I should go faster, I should press the gas until we're both slung back in our seats like they show people in a plane taking off on television.

He keeps tapping out the song. "You're good."

"What about when we get to the highway?"

"Speed limit's fifty-five." He says it like it's nothing and then laughs loudly, a full-on hahaha at me.

I grin, too, though the idea of the highway and the semitrucks that constantly run up and down it makes me nervous. "I could do it. I could," I say. I don't mean it.

"Yeah, yeah, save it for the judge." He lights a smoke, and the smell of burning paper and tobacco covers the smell of the candied vodka. "Don't go telling your mom about this, yeah?"

"Yeah, I won't," I say. I am a good secret keeper, and my dad likes this about me. "Thick as thieves," Mom says about us. I like the way it sounds, the soft and hard syllables together like that.

"I was about your age when my old man put me behind the wheel, you know that?" This is the language of his stories, the opening to whatever story he's planning to spin. Mom calls them tall tales, tells me I should mind less than half of what he says, but the language is special, and it is another one of our secrets. "We were down at McAlester, down there for the prison rodeo—your mama never'd let me bring you to one. They're a hoot, a real good time. Guess she didn't want you hanging around no prison, huh."

Outside the Bronco, it is so dark that the sides of the road seem to come up out of the blackness and spill over us like a covered bridge, like we're shooting through a tunnel of night. The engine roars as we climb a hill, then soar down the other side. A radio jingle plays softly. I wait for him to go on. I don't interrupt when he tells his stories. My silence, too, is a part of the language.

"It got late, and my old man had me watching his buddy's horse trailer so he and them could have a few—did you know he had me riding bulls before I could shave?" I did. "Bulls broke my damn nose more than once. Cain't smell for shit now, huh. But this prison rodeo. It's inside, right, like inside the gates, the barbed wire, and all that. They got guard towers and them guards don't fuck around, right. You're a holler away from death row and some of them cowboys're on the schedule, too. But if you're not a prison cowboy, you're there to ride and get wild and maybe win some money."

An owl swoops into the headlights and just barely misses the windshield. It makes my chest squeeze, but I try not to show it. My dad sucks his teeth in the passenger seat, cracks his window, and pitches the burnt-out stub of his smoke. "Best hope that's the only one we see tonight." He's done with the story, the gears in his head are far past it. He's talking about the owl now, and how owls, like all things, come in threes, and with them comes something bad, something dark. How on the day his old man died, he woke up to three owls sitting pretty on a power line, like they were waiting for him to see them. Old man dropped not an hour later. "Never can tell what's it they want you to know, owls. Could be death, could be a bum radiator cap," he says. "All you're supposed to know is it's coming fast."

He takes a drink, and I see his hand shake from the corner of my eye. I look straight ahead. If his hands get to shaking too bad, I'll have to light his smokes for him. I think how that would work, driving and lighting smokes.

The rain lets up, the wipers squeaking across the windshield. I turn the knob until they slow down. I hear him shift in his seat. "It's just one owl," I say.

"Huh," he says. He lights another smoke, but he lights the wrong end, and it smells like burnt hair and plastic all in one. He curses, pushes it out the window. He drinks. "Only one. Huh."

"I'm sorry," I say. I said the wrong thing by saying anything at all, and I feel like this is what he wants me to say. "Dad? I'm sorry, I didn't mean to interrupt you."

He squeezes my knee, and it makes me press the gas a little harder. The speedometer ticks up to forty-five miles per hour. "I know you didn't, kid," he says, and his breath is sour. His head wobbles from side to side. "You got your mama in you," he says. When he drinks, his drawl, usually a soft twang, sounds like a fiddle in a country song. "You cain't be perfect."

Not too far ahead, headlights tick up and down the highway. It's a little two-lane highway, but it's the easiest way to get between Mom's house and my dad's. About halfway between, there's a Dairy Queen with a ball pit. I'm too old for the ball pit now, but we still meet there, me, my dad, and Mom, every other Friday unless the moon's full. My dad doesn't like to drive under a full moon; he says it's bad luck. Mom says he's superstitious, but she doesn't push it. I didn't see him for a month and half one year. "The moon's getting in the way," he said.

"Your mama," he says, finally. He turns the radio knob again and settles on a country station playing an old Merle Haggard song. Another one of his favorites. "How's she doing?"

Mom says not to talk about her to him. "Your father needs boundaries," she says. "If he has anything to say," she says, "he should ask me." But he doesn't.

"She's okay," I say. "Should I turn around?"

He rolls his window about halfway down and sits there, his hands in his lap, two fingers tracing the rim of the vodka bottle. I imagine for a second that the bottle is singing, but it's just the wind whistling over his unbuckled seat belt. The wind gusts, and the belt snaps a few times. "There's a road coming up. Right. Take it right. You're gonna love this."

"It's late." Last year he got me out of bed, and we drove to Amarillo, Texas to eat at the Big Texan. He ate a seventy-two ounce steak in under an hour, but turns out it's only free if you eat the salad, the bread, the potato, and all of it. He didn't remember it the next day, but we had sundaes from Braum's on the way back and I pinky promised not to tell.

"It'll be early soon," he says. He leans his head back and flecks of rain splash off of him and onto my arm. It is cold and sharp against my skin. "You don't like driving with your old man?"

"I like it fine," I say. I wipe my arm on my pants and swerve the Bronco a little. My dad clicks his tongue at me. "Where're we going, Dad?" He covers the top of my head with his left hand, tangles his fingers in my hair.

"Don't worry about that," he says, leaving his hand on my head. His hand is heavy, but I don't try to shake him off. "Here, turn here."

If I live a hundred years, I think, maybe then I'll know the roads out here like he does. Roads without names, cow paths, shortcuts driven into unfenced pastures; I shiver and do as he says. It's a dirt road, and the rain's made it slick down to the red rock. I go slow, steering around puddles and potholes. Trees line the ditches on either side, and the rain slides off them in heavy swats, pelting the Bronco's steel roof. I know it's steel because my dad told me when he put in the roll cage. He wasn't going to drive no aluminum can piece of shit, he said, only American steel.

"I used to take you out here on nights you were crying," he says. He drinks. "A real screamer you were. Couldn't keep you quiet for nothing. Ain't been back through in a coon's age." He turns the radio volume all the way down. "You hear that?"

I listen. Water sloshes against tires, trees shake in the wind. Softly, uneven thumping beneath the sound of water on water on water. "What is that?"

"You hear it?" he says. "Do you?"

I listen.

"It's bullfrogs."

I brake to a stop when the headlights flicker over a dip in the road. The water looks deep there, twisting and turning in on itself. The thumping is louder, more distinct here.

"Well, go on."

"It's deep."

"Nah, just a little water, kid," he says.

"It looks deep," I say.

"C'mon."

"No. What if we get stuck?"

He opens his door, swinging his bottle wide as he gets out. "Jesus fuck, AJ. Fucking shit."

I dig my foot into the brake pedal. *P* is park, but the shifter won't move for me. There's a trick to it, probably, like that car Mom had that didn't need a key. Mom could put the Bronco in park, I bet. My dad kicks at the headlight and misses, then brings his bottle down on it. The bottle shatters, and he drops the broken neck in the dirt. "Fuck," he says. He looks up and grins. "Oops." He raises his hands, blood on his hands shining brown in the yellow of the headlights. "You hear that, AJ? Do you? Bullfrogs, ya know, ya used to love it here."

I want to get out of the car and go to him. There's probably an emergency brake, but I can't see it in the dark, and I don't even know what to look for. If he walks beyond the headlights, I won't be able to find him. I can't breathe, my throat closed up tight. I bite the inside of my cheek hard to keep my chin from quivering. He walks ahead into the dip, his hair wet and covering his face, his arms out wide and open. The water is up to his knees, but he keeps walking, bringing down the rain. It's like they hear him, the bullfrogs, and they croak louder and louder until I can feel them in my chest. Here and there one hops out of the water before splashing back beneath the surface. There must be thousands of them all around me, hunkered down in the wet dark, talking to one another, telling secrets.

My dad yells something, but it's swallowed by the bullfrogs and echoed back in a chorus.

CALMEZ

Even in the darkness of the closet's interior, Jesco could see that the plant was wilting. The leaves, long and fanned like an open hand, had already begun to curl into fists. He lowered his jeweler's glasses from their place on top of his head, adjusting the elastic band and lenses' magnification ratio. It was too dark to see clearly, but Jesco didn't want to risk throwing the plant's grow cycle by turning on the fluorescent light. With some difficulty, he crouched down and dabbed at its soil. Wiping his fingers on the bib of his overalls, he blew a raspberry.

"What do you want from me?"

The plant, as expected, said nothing, and he stared hard at it through the darkness.

"One of these days, I'm gonna smoke you."

He plucked a joint from behind his ear and lit it, lying back onto the hallway floor. The glasses rested heavily against his face, but he made no move to take them off. The magnification was at 700 percent and he liked the way the spackled ceiling resembled the moon's surface. His glance landed on the fishing wire that ran along the top of the wall; it quivered. The line glinted as it moved just slightly, and Jesco stood up carefully, closing the closet door and pushing the goggles onto his forehead. He crept into the kitchen where the light was better and examined the line carefully. It quivered again, and the bells that hung over the sink clanged loudly. He threw the joint in the sink and himself to the floor. Elbows up, he belly-crawled to the kitchen's south window and peeked over the plywood sill.

His trailer sat facing west on a hill, surrounded on all sides by thick Oklahoma forest. The place was three miles southwest of town; Jesco picked it for its remote location. The unpainted, one-bedroom mobile home rested on cinder blocks up an unpaved, one-lane drive off of County Road 2293. When he moved in, he set up a trip wire alarm around the perimeter. Outside, the fishing wire ran through the underbrush, shallow enough to remain undetected, circling back inside where the lines met at a heavy cluster of bells: copper bells, chiming bells, and a few cowbells. Jesco didn't like surprises, and the plant was nearly five feet tall and a direct violation of his deferred sentence. He wasn't paranoid; he was careful.

Next to the trailer, there was a single light pole that illuminated the small clearing around his place. He scanned the tree line and spotted an unmistakable silhouette: Big Bob's short and stocky frame clamored through the sand plum thicket. The bells rang again, loud enough to be heard outside, and Jesco watched Big Bob perk up at the noise. Big Bob whooped and did a little jig.

"Jessie," Big Bob said. He stomped in a small circle. "Ay, I knew I must have found the place."

Jesco scrambled to his feet and unlatched the door's three bolts and unhooked the chain. He cracked the door just enough to stick his head out.

"Psst, shut the hell up, will you?" Jesco said in a loud hiss. "Get in here, before any of the neighbors hear you."

"Neighbors?" Big Bob wasn't getting any quieter. "I tell you, I walked all around this motherfucker, and you don't have a single one." Big Bob swayed to the trailer's two-tier steps, and Jesco had to offer him an arm up. "What the fuck are you wearing?" Big Bob made a grab for his jeweler's goggles.

"Just get in, Bob," Jesco said. He stuck his head out the door once more and made a quick scan of the yard. His banana-yellow Datsun sat quiet as it always did, a stray cat curled on the hood. Shutting the door, he snapped the locks back into place. "And these"—he pointed to his goggles—"are for work. Probably not much different from what I imagine you had to wear making license plates."

"Joke's on you then," Big Bob said. His wide face was ruddy with liquor. "You should know they stopped having inmates make license plates after all them riots. Besides, my first day as a free man in 1,825 days, and you're cracking jokes about my record? Ice-cold."

"I'm surprised you can count that high. Say now, what's your angle?" Jesco folded his skinny arms across his chest. At his full height, he was a head and a half taller than Big Bob, but Big Bob outweighed him by about a 150 pounds.

"No angle, honest to God." Big Bob vaguely motioned the sign of the cross.

"Don't tell me you were born again in State, huh?" Jesco fished the joint out of the sink; it wasn't too wet. He glanced up and saw Big Bob's face fall, then his lips curled, and he chuckled.

"When'd you get so critical? Sheesh, if I'd wanted someone to question my integrity, I would have tracked down my old lady." Big Bob pulled an unopened fifth of whiskey from his shirt pocket and set it on the kitchen counter. "Can't a man take a seat with an old friend?"

"You're a free man, Big Bob. You can do what you want." Jesco shrugged and lit the joint on the gas stove. He flipped on the stove vent and blew the smoke into it. "But we're not friends. So really, what're you doing in my sand plums?"

Big Bob laughed too loudly and slapped his knee. "Lemme ask you something first, man: What're you doing out here in the sticks? I had to call your mom to get your address, man.

Everybody in town thinks you're at the bottom of Crowder Lake."

"I'm looking to keep it that way, too, so just keep it to yourself, huh?"

"Fine with me, man. Hell, straight outta jail I should be keeping a low profile, too, you know?" Big Bob laughed a little uneasily and unscrewed the whiskey's cap. He took a long pull.

"Tell you the truth, Bob, it's a lot simpler than you think." Jesco swigged off the whiskey bottle and smacked his lips. "I don't have to worry about nobody else, got no law-dog over my shoulder, water's on a well, and if I get hungry, I can go over on the reservation where nobody bothers nobody. It's perfect."

"I suppose that's why you got a Boy Scout's security system out there?" Big Bob raised a heavy brow and sparked a cigarette.

"Junie still in Hydro with the kids?"

"Nah, Junie got herself a new old man," Big Bob said. He rolled his eyes. "Third year in she brought me the papers. Said she couldn't wait five to seven. Her old man paid me 1,200 bucks to sign the kids over to him."

"Shit, dude, don't tell me you signed your kids over." Jesco lit his own cigarette. "I mean, that's low, Bob, low even for you."

Big Bob pulled a fat stack of bills out of his back pocket and laid it on the counter. Jesco held back from picking it up and flipping through the bills. "All twenties. Can't bring money into jail, so it's been sitting at my folks' place in a box for two years," Big Bob grinned. "Guy must be loaded. Only time I ever wished I had more kids."

"You're disgusting," Jesco said. On the other hand, he felt like it was probably a step up for both Junie and her children. Big Bob was a lot of things, but he was definitely not patriarch material. "So now you're a millionaire, big fucking deal. And?"

"Well, now, 1,200 is good for at least a coupla weeks, so I figured I'd hit up my oldest pal and we'd paint the town red," Big Bob said.

"Do you remember *why* you went to jail, Bob?" Jesco asked, flicking ash onto the stove top. "I think it had something to do with—how many DUIs you get again?"

"Six," Big Bob said.

"And first night out of *prison*, you're telling me you want me to facilitate your relapse into criminal society?" Jesco took a sip of the whiskey. "No can do. Your law-dog daddy's retired; he's not gonna bail your ass out again, and if you go down, I'm sure as hell not going with you."

"You used to be fun, Jes," Big Bob said. He was beginning to slur. "We had a ball every night for years, man, fucking *years*."

"Yeah, but then Hippie ran off, Hector and George burnt out, who knows where the fuck Roach is." Jesco paused. "If anybody's at the bottom of Crowder Lake, my money's on Roach. That bastard up and vanished."

"People been watching me take a leak for half a decade, and I'm still not half as paranoid as you," Big Bob said with a laugh. "Let's say we make a wager. We'll flip a coin: Your call, you win, I'll give you the money, all of it," Big Bob stopped to let this thought settle, "but if I win, you come out tonight. I'm still buying, but if I win, you're under contract. No do-overs."

Jesco lit another cigarette as he leaned against the counter. He took a lazy gulp off the bottle and set it back down. He and Big Bob had never been close. If anything, he only tolerated Bob for Hippie's sake, but $1,200 was nothing to shake a stick at. "Deal." No sooner than he'd said it, Big Bob tossed a coin into the air. As it began its downward descent, Big Bob snatched it out of the air and slapped it on the counter. He nodded for Jesco to call it. "Tails."

Big Bob lifted his palm and chuckled loudly. "Heads! Hahaha, looks like we're goin' out tonight, Jesco." He waved the wad of bills. "Don't worry about the tab."

"So where're we headed, honky?" Jesco said flatly.

"I was thinking we'd hit up Calmez," Big Bob said. "What was the name of that one you used to like? Jasmine? Jezebel?" Big Bob howled like a coyote. He slapped his wide palms against the Formica countertop and started bouncing in his chair. Jesco cocked an eyebrow.

"Don't get your hard-on yet; we haven't even left." Jesco knocked back the bottle and gulped down what was left of the whiskey. His Adam's apple bobbed with each swallow until the bottle was empty.

The Calmez Hotel was in Washita City, twenty or so miles west of Jesco's place and just over the county line. When it was built, it was the first and nicest hotel in Washita County. Just off Route 66, Washita City was a city in name only: It held 487 permanent residents and boasted a weekly newspaper. In a small town that saw little traffic, the Calmez Hotel had more than seventy-five rooms. An old, neon tube light spelling *Calmez Hotel* still hung above the bowed aluminum awning. The lights had been burnt out as long as anyone could remember, though, and a frayed electrical cord dangled above the entrance. The whole town knew the place was a whorehouse, but half the county's deputies were among the best customers.

Big Bob wanted to drive, and against his better judgment, Jesco let him flip the damn coin for it. Big Bob called it and won, excitedly jumping into the driver's seat. He took the roundabout way of getting there, swinging wide turns and straddling the middle of the road. In the passenger seat, Jesco gripped the dashboard until his fingers cramped. The Datsun's headlights veered onto Gary Street, flashing across the face of the dilapidated hotel. The bricks were beginning to chip toward the top, and the Art Deco façade had already come off in spots, crumbling to the street six floors below. There were a couple bums passed out around the doors, but for the most part, the Calmez looked empty.

Big Bob let the truck glide to a stop directly in front, slamming the emergency brake on. The jolt sent Jesco's forehead crashing against the windshield. He cursed and recoiled, cupping his head. He felt his heartbeat in his forehead.

"Is it bleeding? Aw, fuck, Big Bob," Jesco said as his eyes watered.

"Nah, you're fine. We're here." Big Bob smacked him on the back, and Jesco grunted. "Come on, Jessie! I've been waiting five long years for this." He hopped out of the truck and slapped a beat against the truck bed as he made his way around. He went right in, not bothering to wait for Jesco to follow.

The interior of the Calmez hadn't been redone since before World War II, and it was apparent. Maroon and gold triangles patterned the carpet, and the staircase retained its brass balustrades and mahogany rail. The railing was nicked all the way up, like notches on a gun's handle. Full of confidence, Big Bob sauntered up to the reception desk. A chicken wire cage was rigged up around it, and someone filled the holes with bits of different colored tissue paper. The desk was elevated, coming to just below Big Bob's chin, and he puffed out his chest and propped his elbows on the counter. Behind the desk was a thin, dark-skinned man in big, black-rimmed Ray-Bans. His hair was slicked back in a wave, and it shone in the dim light.

"What can I do for you, sir?" the man said.

"Guess and I bet you get it," Big Bob replied. "I'm here for pussy, my man. Plain and simple."

"That don't mean a whole lot here," the man said. "It takes all kinds, right? You got a preference?"

"Any kind of pussy's fine with me." Big Bob slipped a twenty dollar bill beneath the chicken wire screen.

"You one of them doll freaks? I don't get it, but you know," the man said, "do you."

Jesco watched Big Bob puff himself up like he used to when he was trying to look bigger. "I just got out, man," Bob said.

"Prison, huh?" The man behind the counter laughed. "You ain't the only one." He pushed a button on the switchboard and mumbled something into a microphone. "Fourth floor, room twenty-two."

Big Bob whooped and headed for the stairs. He was doing the same jig he'd done in Jesco's front yard. Once they left his trailer, Big Bob was a man of singular intention. Jesco watched Big Bob's backside disappear around the corner. Jesco shoved his hands in his pockets and paced in front of the wire cage. The man behind the desk cleared his throat. Jesco turned toward him slowly.

"What can I do for you?" He lowered his sunglasses and eyed Jesco's pupils. "We don't want no tweakers in here, so if that's your deal then I have to ask you get the hell out. Nothing personal, understand, it's just bad for business." He smiled amiably.

"Nah, no," Jesco waved him off. "No thanks, man. I'm just waiting on a friend."

"In that case, if you're inclined to stay, could I interest you in some, per se, alternative pastimes?" The lamp caught the man's gold ring and reflected against the wire. "A gentleman friend, perhaps?"

Jesco's hands dug deeper into his pockets. "Ah, no, that's not really my bag either."

"Which way do you swing, then?"

He stopped pacing, "Actually I'm just gonna sit down."

"Anybody ever tell you you look like one of them tobacco store Indians?"

"Never heard that one," Jesco said. He took a seat on the only empty bench in the lobby, closest to the desk. His head throbbed, and he felt a black eye ruminating beneath his skin. Surveying the lobby, he saw the waiting room's other occupants. Besides the drunks and junkies, someone left a baby car seat with a blanket in the shape of a frog thrown over it. Cautiously, Jesco lifted the blanket and peered inside. His heart jumped: empty.

"Hey," Jesco said. "You know what happened to the baby?"

"What'd you say?"

"The baby. The one whose car seat that is, and the blanket," Jesco said. "It's gotta belong to somebody."

The man peered over the desk. "Fuck if I know, man. Can't see shit from back here."

"Yeah, but you gotta notice somebody bringing a baby in, right? I mean it's not like babies just walk in all the time, right?" Jesco said. He was beginning to think the man in the cage thought he was hysterical. Who would bring a baby to a brothel?

"Look, man, if I had a dollar for every time a baby came through that door—" the man stopped himself. "I wouldn't be a rich man, but I'd sure as hell get a good roll out of it."

Jesco didn't have a chance to respond as a thump resounded upstairs, quickly followed by a distant door slam and the heavy stomp of footsteps. Jesco knew it was Big Bob before he came into view. His glance darted from the baby seat to the man behind the desk. Big Bob roared down the stairs. "I didn't get my rocks off!" He heaved a fist into the wall. He marched up to the reception desk and stuck his fingers through the wire. His weight tugged at the fence's structure, and it bowed in the middle. "Your bitch didn't let me finish."

"Problems?" The man behind the counter pursed his lips and steadied a cool gaze at Big Bob. "You know they say that boozing makes you soft, and by the smell of your breath and the look on your face, I'd say that's about right."

"Motherfucker, you gave me a bum whore." Big Bob shook the wire cage. "I want my money back."

"Sorry, no refunds," the man said, pushing his sunglasses up.

"You little bastard—" Big Bob punched the wire cage and almost instantly, the man held the mouth of a .38 pistol through the wire, aimed directly at Big Bob's temple. Jesco got to his feet.

"I said we don't give no refunds."

Big Bob choked, and a gob of spit dribbled out of his mouth.

"Hey, hey, look, it's fine, man, I'll take him outta here," Jesco said as he laid a hand on Big Bob's shoulder, steering him toward the door. "It's fine, man, no big deal, it's fine."

The man didn't lower the gun. "You keep that fool outta here, understand?"

"Sure thing, sure thing, no problems here," Jesco said.

"And take your baby shit, too."

Big Bob moved easily beneath the pressure on his shoulder, like a puppet to which Jesco held the strings. As the door closed behind them, Jesco saw the man reclaim his seat behind the damaged cage. "You're still driving, you ass."

Big Bob plodded dumbly to the driver's side and got in, Jesco sliding in opposite. There was a little grease mark on the windshield from Jesco's forehead. He patted the dashboard.

"Let's go," Jesco said. "Get gone."

"She looked just like my old lady, man," Big Bob drawled as he turned the ignition and shifted the car into first gear. "Just like her. It wasn't, though. I asked."

"That why you couldn't get it up?" Jesco said.

Four miles shy of Jesco's dirt drive, he heard a low grating sound that seemed to come from beneath him. He glanced back over his shoulder and saw nothing but darkness and the road rolling behind them. As the road widened, the grating grew louder, and Jesco squirmed in his seat. He cracked his door open and stole a look outside. The passenger's side of the truck was entirely up against the recessed curb, the tires grating along cement.

"Big Bob!" Turning to his friend, he saw the man curled up against the steering wheel, drool trailing onto the floorboard. Jesco right hooked him as hard as he could. In the rearview mirror, the reflection of a black-and-white caught his eye. A sheriff's sedan began to gain on them.

"Motherfucker, wake up!" Jesco hit him again, and Big Bob sat up with a groan. "Pull the car over, pull the car over."

Big Bob groggily complied, and Jesco saw the sedan's lights go on. Big Bob was probably seeing double and didn't seem to notice; he swayed woozily and came to rest with his forehead against the steering wheel.

Jesco threw open the passenger door and bailed, using the curb as a springboard into the scrub that lined the rural road. He ran. His long legs took leaping strides as he dodged decaying logs and spindly sand plum trees. The sheriff's revolving lights reflected against the wide, black sky, and he kept running in the opposite direction. When he did risk a look back, he saw Big Bob's stout frame bent over the Datsun's hood. A hundred or so yards ahead, he saw the silhouettes of trees. A light flickered against them, and he was sure the sheriff had sent someone in the brush after him. Running faster, he veered northwards to the creek, the thorns and brambles scratching at his face and arms. Even as his side cramped and his stomach heaved, he kept running, and he ran until he came over the backside of the hill. He stopped short, panting, and his dirty trailer seemed to glow under its yellow lamp. He took a few stiff steps forward, and he heard the bells going off inside. He tapped his feet and the bells rang again. Thousands of stars shone down on his little plot.

SHELLS II

Our room is around the back of the motel, away from the highway floodlights. Hiram and Baby are sleeping in the backseat by the time we pull up, and Mama carries Baby while Daddy slings Hiram over his shoulder like a sack of flour. I walk myself. I'm grown enough to see the motel before we even get there, before Mama's even started folding up her quilts. Quilts is about the only thing she brings anymore.

This last house I kind of liked, but once Mama and Daddy decided it was time to leave, Daddy pulled the stove off the wall for its copper. Left a mess, dust and plaster all over the floor, but the landlord's a real prick. When Mama finally got Hiram and Baby and Daddy to *just get in the damn car already, we ain't got all day,* I said I had to pee and ran back in, though the water'd been shut off all week.

The house wasn't empty, just empty of us. The mattress with the busted coil was against the front window and a pot of macaroni and cheese was on a shelf. I hopped over cups and old clothes into the kitchen. There was this knob on one of the drawers that I liked, a little painted metal flower, and I'd been working on loosening that screw. No time for that now. I sat on the floor and put my feet up against the drawer, trying to wrench it out. I wanted it.

"Frankie!" The car horn honked out front, two short beeps, not enough to get anyone's attention.

"Gimme a minute," I hollered.

I kicked the drawer as hard as I could, the wood cracking and, finally, splinters and all, the flower was mine. Brushing it off as best I could, I put my flower in my pocket.

One thing I don't like about Mama's wandering bones is that we always drive at night. Hiram's only six and Baby's just a baby, so they sleep, but me, I see the road. This time, I think we're heading east, but it could be south. If the sun were up, I'd know. We're between towns, so there's nothing but the blinking lights of the wind farm and the occasional floodlights of an oil rig. The windows are down, and it feels like we're driving through stars.

"Where we going?"

"We're just gonna go until we can't no more, punkin," Mama says. "Maybe we'll find a place where you can get back in school, huh? Wouldn't that be nice?"

"Nice as a kick in the ass," I say.

"Watch your language."

I think it's the routine that drives them nuts, Mama and Daddy. It starts with a hiss in the blood, then a settling feeling that strikes low, deep in the gut, weighing you down like a cinderblock. Sometimes I feel it in my palms, like when your hand goes to sleep and it's just waking up. This last time I knew it was coming when Mama started talking about investing in a nice set of silverware. She was doing the dishes. Washing those pink plastic forks Daddy swiped from the Party Mart. She had suds up to her elbows and maybe she looked happy, but every time she brought the sponge out the water, she'd blink real fast like she'd caught smoke in her eye.

The room is like all the rooms: varnished table with a plastic gold-colored inlay down the legs, cheap varnished chairs, a nightstand, a TV, and a large bed with a scratchy, pink and blue comforter. Mama and Daddy will sleep with Hiram and Baby, and I'll get a pallet on the floor. At least this room has carpet, even if it's thin and has a deep tread into the bathroom. While Mama settles Hiram and Baby in the bed, Daddy clicks on the TV and throws himself into a chair. It's the Weather Channel. He takes out the little bottle he keeps in his pocket and takes a drink, smacking his lips.

I make my place on the floor and open up the sack of boiled eggs Mama made for the trip. She left the shells on because she knows I like to roll each egg between my palms, cracking the shell until it peels away in one solid piece. I do this now with two of the eggs and spread the shells out side by side. They make me think of earthquakes, something I've only seen on TV. I imagine the earth opening up beneath me, swallowing me into its yolk, and then I crush the shells beneath my thumbs. The dust feels good on my fingers, but Mama swats my hand.

"What're you doin'? Making a mess already?" Mama says.

"I'm eating, duh."

I don't look at her as I say it. She grabs my arm and digs her nails in like she does when she's angry. She lets me really feel the pink half-moons forming on my arm, and she talks through her teeth. *"Frances Marie, you pick that shit up now."*

She lets me go, and I stuff a whole egg in my mouth. "They on the sheets, it's easy," I mumble, talking through egg and shame. I sweep the crumbled pieces into my hand and toss them into the trash. Mama doesn't look at me as she lies down, just motions for Daddy to hand her the remote and starts flipping through. The TV wobbles into focus on each channel, and she settles on *Elvira: Mistress of the Dark.* I've seen it before—Daddy and me watched it at this one motel that had concrete floors. Mama takes a boiled egg from the bag and carefully, delicately peels the shell off in pieces, dropping the bits into the garbage.

She glances at me from the corner of her eye. I know this is just for show. She's probably not even hungry.

Mama told me once that she never really considered herself the mothering type until she had me, and then the "surprises," meaning Hiram and Baby. *Surprise* is just her way of saying *accident* or *mistake*. It's moments like this when I think what she must have been like before we came along, when it was just her and Daddy, living like we do now, I guess. Could she really have changed that much? On the other hand, Daddy says that people don't really change; they just get better at hiding what they are.

I wake up and *Elvira: Mistress of the Dark* is still on, and Daddy's dozing in the chair, feet propped up on the little table, an unlit cigarette dangling from his mouth. Mama and the babies are curled up and around one another: Mama, then Hiram, then Baby. Hiram and Baby have her nose and her so-black-it's-blue hair, and she lets Hiram wear his hair long so the image isn't a stretch.

On TV, Elvira's finally got that show in Vegas she's worked so hard for, and she does this thing where she spins these black boobie tassels around and around just by popping her shoulders back and forth. I thought it was a little weird the first time I saw it, but now I'm more impressed than anything else. My boobs just started growing, and they're nothing like hers. Mama called mine mosquito bites once, and I told her hers looked like socks filled with sand. I felt bad about that.

Something shakes the wall behind the TV, and I jump. The digital clock on the nightstand says 4:43 AM. The highway hums outside, and I listen. I expect to hear bed springs next, like I've heard before, but the quiet makes me clench my hands into fists. I watch Elvira shake around some more, applauded by her punk-rock poodle, and then the wall shakes so hard that the picture fuzzes out and Elvira's lost in a gray and blue swarm that rides up and down the screen. This one wakes up Daddy, and he pops out of the chair, bleary-eyed but ready.

"What the fuck was that?" he whispers. He doesn't realize I am awake.

"There's something in the wall," I say.

"What are you doing awake?" The wall shakes again, this time with the sound of glass shattering. "Never mind. It's not our business."

He sits back in the chair and lights the smoke, pulling the plastic ashtray across the table with his thumb. The TV shudders back into focus, and the credits are rolling.

"What were you watching?"

"*Elvira.*"

"Oof, sorry I missed that," he says. "But you shouldn't be watching that."

"I've seen it before," I say, "with you."

"Fair enough."

The room next door thumps and rumbles. It reminds me of the dryers at coin laundries. When we got here, I saw that the windowsill of room eleven was lined with little ceramic figurines—dogs, mostly, but there was a six-inch high unicorn in the center position. The curtains were drawn, the little corgis and cocker spaniels pressed up against the glass like the display in a gift shop. It was out of place, all the little knickknacks set up like that where no one would ever see them. If Hiram had been awake, he would've asked or maybe even begged for one. He liked trinkets like that, and even though he was almost six and a half, he still didn't understand the difference between theirs and ours, them and us. Whenever we stopped at gas stations we had to watch him. He would stuff his pockets if he thought he could. I finger the flower knob in my pocket.

It used to surprise me that people lived in the places we stopped. I imagined they came to these places like we did, passing through, and something held them up, like they were waiting for something that had yet to come. Or maybe they got tired, or maybe they really did love their motel room, though I saw little to love and even less worth staying for.

I sit up when I hear a soft knock on our door. I look at Daddy and he looks at me, like neither of us are quite sure what to do. He goes to the door and, hand over the switchblade he keeps tucked into the back of his pants, opens it just a crack. Hurrying to my feet, I peek around his elbow.

It is a woman with stringy, bleach-blond hair and thick eyeshadow around her eyes. Her left cheek blooms purple and snot drips onto her upper lip. She cradles a baby not much younger than Baby in her arms, and the baby fusses and pushes against her.

"I'm real sorry to bother y'all," she says as she jostles the baby, "but my mama and my boyfriend are fighting, and I can't get'em away from each other with this little one in there. Could you—"

Mama presses my head away with the flat of her palm and opens the door wide. Sometimes I forget what a light sleeper she is, and my ear burns where she smashed it.

"Come on in, honey," Mama says, "you sit down now. That cheek don't look too good."

The woman sits in Daddy's chair, and in the light she doesn't look much older than me, but the lines around her mouth say different. She tries to smile but it comes out crooked because of her cheek.

"It's nothing, really," she says. The baby in her arms begins to cry and she gets this panicky look and starts to rock the baby, but she rocks it too hard, and even I know that she won't be able to calm it.

Mama goes to her and takes the baby, propping it against her shoulder the way she does when she's burping Baby. "What's his name, hon?" Mama eyes this woman the way she does cops, park rangers, and social workers, even though it's obvious she's none of those.

"Elijah," she says. "Elijah. He's not mine, though. He belongs to this lady at my work. She asked me to keep him tonight."

There's a crash and scream next door, and the TV screen flickers. The girl's face tightens like a coyote's on the side of the interstate. She's afraid.

"I'm sorry—real sorry. To ask strangers," she begins, "it's just I don't want him to get hurt." Behind her I catch Mama and Daddy shooting each other looks.

"What about your mama?" I ask, and I get a swat to the thigh.

"They're both drunk, and they usually don't hurt each other too bad but . . ."

"Want I should call the law?" Daddy asks. He's by the phone, but he doesn't lift it off its cradle. My palms itch; I wonder if someone else will call the cops and how quickly we can drive away from this place.

"No, please, don't," she says quickly. Mama frowns. She's sized this girl up, and she's not liking what she sees. "No cops. I'm gonna go back over there, I can settle them down. Could you just keep him for me? Just for a minute?"

Daddy looks at Mama, and she nods. Mama rubs the baby Elijah's back, and he's cooing against her neck. "Alright," she says.

"Thank you, I'll be back as soon as I can," the girl says. She's got a bounce in her step when she makes for the door. As it shuts behind her, another muffled cry springs from behind the wall.

Hiram sleeps like the dead, but the commotion's woken up Baby, and he begins to cry. I can almost see his baby eyes narrow when he spots Mama cradling this stranger.

"Oh, c'mere, sweet Baby," Mama coos, "Mama's here."

She passes Elijah off to me before taking up Baby, and I hold this stranger baby out in front of me like a puppy. He's skinny for a baby, and I sit him upright on my lap and bounce him on my knee.

"Here, sit across from me," Mama says. "Maybe they'll play with each other."

Daddy lights a smoke and changes the station to the Weather Channel. He turns up the volume, and the easy, instrumental soft rock half drowns the blows from next door. The week's forecast is high nineties, strong winds, little chance of rain.

I scoot to the edge of the bed and sit cross-legged, Elijah just in front of me, my hands holding up his curved little back. The flower in my pocket digs into my thigh as I try to keep him from toppling over. He leans forward heavily as if his head is weighing him down. Baby, who is bigger, does the same, except it's just a means to swipe at Elijah's head. Baby lets out a squawk and pushes forward again, his legs propelling him. His nails scrape against Elijah's head before I can pull him out of reach, and Elijah begins to cry. It occurs to me that Baby's never seen another like him and knowing he's not the only one must be terrifying.

"I don't think he likes him."

"They're babies, Frankie," Mama says. "They don't like anything."

For a while after Hiram was born, I stayed with Daddy's friend Manuel and his old lady, Gizzard. Mama told me not to call her that, that her name was LeAnn, but Gizzard didn't mind, so I called her that out of Mama's earshot. Manuel and Gizzard were bikers, and Manuel was president of his club, the Dead Rats. Their patch was a poison symbol with a rat skull, and Manuel never went anywhere without his club cut. He tried to get Daddy to prospect every time we visited, but Daddy always said no.

They lived in a little farmhouse in the middle of nowhere with a bunch of no-name dogs, and when we visited, Gizzard would make up the screened porch in the back like it was my own room. Manuel took apart cars for a living, and at any given time there might be five or six old frames I could play in. Gizzard took me on her bike once, but I burned my leg on the exhaust pipe, and Mama said no after that.

It was cold the day we pulled into their driveway, coming or going from one of the somewheres I don't remember. My coat was a season too small, and my wrists ached. Mama and Daddy didn't talk as they drove or even listen to the radio, which I remember thinking was weird, especially as we were going to stay with our friends.

They didn't say how long they'd be gone. They didn't even come into the house or unbuckle Hiram from his car seat. When they each crouched down and hugged me, I felt like a handshake would've fit a little better. Gizzard put her hands on my shoulders and pressed her fingers into my collarbones. They didn't look at me, Mama or Daddy, as they got back in the car. Gizzard steered me into the house like a buggy, sitting me down at her high, wooden table. She gave me a glass of something called Ovaltine that looked and smelled like chocolate milk, but it left a thick dust on my tongue, so I spat it on the table and told her it tasted like horse piss. It was something Daddy said once. She asked me if I wanted a birthday party, even though Daddy took me to Chuck-E-Cheese for my fourth birthday some months before.

I can't say for how long I stayed there. Mama and Daddy called sometimes, but they always sounded so far away that it felt like it couldn't be them I was talking to because that would mean they'd really gone. I remember being outside a lot, the smell of wet dirt in the air after it rains. I must have been too young for school. I don't remember going. But a school bus bumped along the road twice a day. Sometimes the kids on the bus would wave if I was out in the field, climbing over some frame or chasing the dogs. A couple times, a few boys spit out the window, too far away to even come close to me but near enough that I threw rocks at them.

Gizzard caught me the last time. She let out a shrill whistle from the porch, a trick I knew she picked up from Mama, and even from across the field I could tell she was angry. I loped back to the porch, my wide step trying to fake calm or carelessness. Gizzard put a stop to that right quick. As soon as I was in arm's reach, she snatched my elbow and tried to whip me around to spank me, but something was off, and I twisted but my arm didn't. I felt my elbow slide into itself and out, like a sprung hinge on a door, and at first, it just felt icy cold then, when she let my arm go and I couldn't hold it up, it burned from the inside.

Gizzard cried. She cried, and I cried, and she said we'd have to wait for Manuel to get home. When he finally did, he drove us to the hospital two counties over, told the lady at the desk I fell out of a tree. Driving back, Gizzard cried some more, though it sounded like she was screaming underwater. I'd gotten a shot of something before the doctor put my elbow back together, and it made me too sleepy to listen. I'd watched the doctor do it, but it was almost like a dream: the click of my bones together like Legos. On the way back, Manuel's voice carried like a lawn mower's roar over the soft hum of the road. I slept better in the backseat of that car than I had since I'd been dropped off.

143

The next evening, Mama and Daddy pulled up the drive, the sideboards of our car caked in red dirt. Mama barely looked at my slinged arm, barely looked at me at all. Hiram had a full head of hair, his fat baby face had taken on some of the shapes and angles of Mama's. He gurgled in his car seat. I climbed in next to him, and Daddy restarted the car.

"Seat belts," Mama said.

There's shouting now, louder than the Weather Channel's version of "Landslide." Hiram and Baby are both half asleep, their eyes open but not moving, lying still on the big bed. Hiram's lips pucker like a fish, his tongue poking through the gap in his teeth; he was on the bottle too long. He pops his thumb in his mouth and sucks noisily.

Mama paces, bouncing Elijah on her hip. He cries in short, gasping breaths, his face all twisted up and red. I wonder what his mother does. "I'm gonna call them," she says. "This is fucking stupid. I can't listen to this all night."

"It's not our business, Jemma," Daddy says. "Leave it be. We don't want this to come back on us." He sips from his little bottle. "We can ride it out."

"You don't think she'd really not come back, do you?" she says. "Too nice. Shouldn't have been nice. We've got enough on our own."

Daddy lights up again, relighting the stub of a cigarette that'd gone out, and he exhales through his nose. His lips twitch beneath his mustache. "Oh, come on."

"Here, Frankie," she says. "You take this." She hands Elijah to me, and I lay him down on his belly over a pillow. He still cries, but he's not as insistent as before. The shouting is just background noise, like static on the radio. On the TV, a pretty blond delivers a report on riptides in South Carolina. An uptick in riptides has caused seven drownings so far.

"Didn't you say you always wanted to see Myrtle Beach?" Daddy says. Mama swats his knee.

When Baby was born, we were staying with Manuel and Gizzard again. We didn't see them so much after Mama and Daddy picked me up, but eventually we circled back, probably because we didn't have anywhere else. Gizzard was really nice to me, so I cussed and spat at her whenever I could. Mama saw it, but she didn't stop me.

The night Baby was born, they were playing cards, everyone drinking but Mama, and her water broke right there in the kitchen. Hiram was coloring on the floor, and some of it soaked into his coloring book. Daddy had to scoop him up and take him outside while Gizzard helped Mama into the bathroom. Baby came out in the bathtub an hour later, fat, hungry, and screaming. While Mama rested, Gizzard kept Baby happy, changing him, feeding him, bathing him. I didn't hate her when I watched her with him. She always wanted a little boy, she told me, swaddling Baby up in a cotton blanket. I told her she could keep this one, if she wanted.

"Oh, hon," she said. "Some of us are just meant to be aunties. That's the facts." She used the soft brush to push Baby's hair across his forehead. "When I was your age, I wanted five babies. With that many you'd never have to worry about them being lonely."

A week later, we were back in the car, pointed east or maybe north, Manuel and Gizzard waving at us, sitting side by side on their white porch swing, their band of dogs chasing us down the drive.

When Mama gets upset, she paces and she does this thing with her hands where they flutter at her sides like hummingbirds. She used to hide it, sitting on her hands in a chair or in the car.

Here, in the little matchbook motel room, the quickness in her hands makes my skin bristle. I press my palm into my thigh; the hard edges of the metal flower in my pocket dig into my skin. I imagine a perfect flower stamped into my leg, a perfect, purple scar blooming. I flinch: A wood splinter found its way through my jeans and into my palm. There's not much blood. Just enough to leave a pin-sized bloom on the blue denim.

"Come sit down, hon," Daddy says. A bedspring bounces in the room next door. "They'll wear themselves out soon."

"Well, we've got to do something," Mama presses.

"What, you want me to go kick his ass?" She gives him a look and Daddy snorts. "No, sorry," he says. "It's not good for anyone if we go over there."

Wood splinters next door, and this time, the screaming doesn't stop.

A man on television explains that a tornado forms when the cool air of an updraft meets the warm air of a downdraft. The video playing behind him shows a Jeep sliding across a four-lane highway.

"Do something."

Daddy shakes his head. He looks old in the yellow light of the lamps, and from my place on the floor I can see the shadows running beneath his cheekbones. He rubs his eyes with both hands and sighs, putting his hands out like he's praying. He doesn't look at Mama, but I catch his eye for a flickering second. He opens his mouth a little in a way that feels sad. Mama just stands over him, her jaw set tight. The muscles in her neck play like piano strings.

I saw Mama fight once, with Gizzard, but she didn't know I could see her. It was somewhere between Vinita and Chouteau, some big thing Manuel was throwing for the Dead Rats. It was too hot to stay in the tent. All the grown-ups were drunk and more than a few were laid out with half their clothes off in the grass. Gizzard must've said something that set Mama off; Mama was on her like a dog on a rabbit. It took three men, Manuel included, to pull her off. She chipped Gizzard's tooth on her knuckles. Daddy told me later that they fight like sisters.

But Mama isn't flaring mad like that now. Her face is hard, even as another crash echoes through the thin walls. Time feels slower, but I know it's not because I don't think anyone can scream that long. "Give me your knife," she says. Daddy hands it over, the blade still clipped into the handle.

"The clasp is sticky," he says. She gives him a short nod.

"What are you gonna do, Mama?" I say. She looks at me like she's just remembered I'm there and then turns to the door. The screams have stopped; only a thin whine, interrupted by bursts of coughing. The handle on our door twitches. Mama opens Daddy's knife and, with the blade in her left hand, she jerks open the door.

There in the door frame, stark against the yellow security lamps in the parking lot, is a man. Even shadowed, he's pale and thin, like a bad cartoon. For a second, he starts and stares at Mama. His eyes shine so bright it's hard to imagine he can see anything with them. Mama raises the knife. She screams. She screams louder than the people next door have all night, waving the knife wildly, stamping her feet, shaking her hair. It only takes about three seconds of this before the man sort of shudders and takes off, tearing through the parking lot as fast as his legs can carry him. Once he's gone, Mama stops screaming and brushes the hair back from her face. I go to the door and watch him run. He doesn't have any shoes on. Mama puts the knife on the table and sits on the side of the bed. She puts her head in her hands, and her shoulders begin to shake. At first it looks like she's crying, but she starts snorting, and then she's laughing hysterically, giggling. Daddy starts to laugh, so I start laughing, too, and the babies, startled by Mama's tantrum, stop fussing.

When they've finished, Daddy scoops up Elijah and takes him out of our room. The voices next door are nicer, quiet. One even laughs. Mama sets about getting Baby's bag and some of our odds and ends back out to the car. Hiram sleeps with his eyes open again; he can sleep through anything.

The weight of the metal flower feels good in my pocket. I feel like I haven't slept in days, almost giddy. When Daddy comes back, he and Mama hustle the little ones into the car. Hiram they let lie on the floor, curled into the floorboard. I'm last, like I'm always last. "C'mon then, Frankie," Daddy says. He shoos me out of the room, shutting the door behind us. I glance at the window to the room next door: The trinkets are gone, except for one ceramic corgi. The figurine has a chip in its ear, giving it a cockeyed look.

I climb into the backseat and rest my head against the window. The glass is cool on my forehead. Daddy turns the ignition and off we go, headed east or west or I don't know. I keep my eye on the horizon, waiting for the sun to tell me where we're going.

WANT

We want everything, and we take it. We do it easily, and we do it often. We do it in plain sight. We accumulate things for the sake of having things; each time sates us for a while, but the want creeps like ivy. The things we take are an ointment, and there is no cure.

We are six years old, and our mother still cannot tell us apart. She's always at work or night school, and we have grown used to being alone. As a rule, we are not supposed to leave our apartment, but the air conditioner is broken, and the apartment is sweltering. Popsicles would be nice, we think, so we are digging in the couch cushions and under the television. We find thirteen cents, a lollipop stick, and a dead beetle.

We leave anyway and walk the three blocks to the Gas-Em-Up. The store has an ice machine that, when we open its doors wide, feels like walking into a glacier. We do this for a while until the clerk tells us to leave. He points to the sign in the window, *No Shirt, No Shoes, No Service*, and then snorts incredulously at our feet. Our toes are nearly black. A man wheels in a dolly, and the clerk forgets about us. We go into the sun, where the heat mirages make wavering pools above the cement.

A Hostess truck blocks the sidewalk, and we are angry with this man, though we are not sure why. The back of the truck is open, and we recognize the names of things we are rarely allowed to have: Twinkies, HoHos, Zingers—the works. We work together, and we work quickly, loading our arms with as many as we can carry. We make off with eight boxes. The sidewalk is hot, and we run as fast as we can.

In our apartment, we empty all the boxes onto the rug and gorge ourselves, one cake at a time. We eat and we eat until our stomachs are distended and we ache with sugar, but we are careful: We throw away the evidence before we hear our mother's key in the door. She sees our pale, nauseated faces and keeps us out of school for the rest of the week.

The Raspberry Zinger is one of Hostess' less popular snack cakes. The outside of the moist cake is covered in raspberry syrup and coconut flakes. This mixture is bitingly sweet, and the coconut flakes taste like paper. Like its brother snack, the Twinkie, Zingers are also cream filled. Ostensibly vanilla-flavored, the cream has a distinctly chemical aftertaste, like a fluoride treatment at the dentist's. The Raspberry Zinger is superior to other kinds of Zingers because it doesn't pretend to adhere to any existing standards of taste. A watermelon lollipop tastes nothing like a watermelon, and it isn't expected to. It is in this way that the Raspberry Zinger triumphs over Devil's Food and Iced Vanilla Zingers. Expectations are low, and the sugar content is high.

We are twelve and spend our days at the public pool across town. We ride our bikes or walk, but we are always there when the gates are opened, and we leave only when the whistle blows for Adult Swim. Our skin is dark like wet soil, and the chlorine bleaches the tips of our hair. Our eyes are perpetually red.

Today we ride our bikes home, throwing our towels in the white wicker baskets that sit on our handlebars. It is nearly nine o'clock, but the sun still sits in the sky, though its heat has diminished. We cut across the park and take the jogging trail under the bridge, where it curves like an on-ramp into our neighborhood. Our neighborhood is dotted with churches-cum-soup kitchens and tonight we stop at the Calvary Hill Methodist Church and Outreach Center. Our mother comes here once a month for the food distribution, and we have long stopped accompanying her.

The Outreach Center opens into an alleyway. We ditch our bikes behind a dumpster and try the door: unlocked. We are practically invited in by the hum of the power line overhead. It's dark inside, and we quickly make our way to the kitchen behind the auditorium. Flyers tacked to a corkboard on the kitchen's door advertise AA and NA meetings, along with a bright poster for the church's monthly raffle. We take the poster.

At first glance, the kitchen is bare, but we know better. We comb the cabinets carefully, setting our chosen items on the counter. We choose a six-pack of paper towels, a tub of Ovaltine, three packets of yeast, a can of sweet potatoes, a Tupperware half filled with pickled okra, and a handheld AM/FM radio. We rearrange the shelves, obscuring the holes where our things used to be. We are confident that the volunteers will not notice.

The paper towels are too large for our baskets, so we rip into the plastic packaging and salvage three rolls. The rest we toss in the dumpster. With our beach towels wrapped around our chests like bandoliers, we secure our bounty. We tune the AM/FM radio to the local pop station and ride home to Top 40 Hits.

Bounty bills itself as "The Quicker Picker Upper," and according to Consumer Reports, it's justified. Bounty is the best-selling brand in the United States, and Procter & Gamble couldn't be more pleased. Though Bounty may cost a bit more, you're really paying for quality. Other paper towels, especially the generics, have less than a third of the absorbency of Bounty's DuraTowel while their ExtraSoft Paper Towels come in a smooth second. Since 1837, Procter & Gamble has amassed a portfolio that includes twenty-five different brand names worth more than a billion dollars each. They are the company that brought us Crisco, Ivory soap, Charmin Toilet Paper (another leader in its category), and Pampers disposable diapers. In the late seventies, they also released an ultra-absorbent synthetic tampon that ultimately caused toxic shock syndrome. After eight months of damning reports from the CDC and thirty-eight documented deaths, Procter & Gamble issued a recall. The tampons were called Rely.

We are fourteen and have just recently started wearing bras. After school, we walk down Main Street, trawling the thrift stores that pepper the block. We avoid Next-To-Nu; the place is always empty, and the clerk there hovers over us, suggesting demure pant suits and sweaters only an octogenarian would love. She calls us "hon," and we hate her.

The Goodwill is our favorite. The aisles are overstocked and narrow, and each rack is piled high with knickknacks, plate sets, and stuffed animals, so it's impossible to see from one aisle to the next. The Goodwill is our treasure chest. We move comfortably down each aisle, filling our arms with shirts, dresses, and sweaters until we can barely hold them all. These are our decoys.

The dressing rooms are at the back and without doors. Each closet-sized stall is closed off by a shower curtain—suspiciously secondhand, with old mold stains climbing up the polyester fabric. We dump our haul on the benches and put on the clothes we actually want: a cotton fringe top, a satin blouse, two T-shirts, and a swimsuit with the tags still on. Our loose sweaters hide our bodies easily, and the cashier thanks us as we leave. We leave the rest of the clothes in a heap on the dressing room floor.

The swimsuit is a high-rise two-piece that originally retailed for $29.95. The tags jangle from a simplified zip tie. Black and white chevron stripes cover the wide bottoms, the pattern ending just at the hips. The chevron arrows dive into the crotch and emerge on the other side, creating the illusion of an hourglass figure from the back. The top is a simple string bikini, two impossibly small black triangles that would flatter a B cup at best.

The swimsuit was assembled by Delta Galil Industries, an Israeli corporation with factories in the West Bank, Thailand, Ukraine, the United Kingdom, and Pakistan, among others, though the swimsuit very well may have come from any of their subcontractors in China, India, Bangladesh, Vietnam, or Sri Lanka.

We are sixteen and at odds with our bodies. We smoke cigarettes as we walk down alleyways and empty streets, skipping school for the umpteenth time. The cigarettes settle our stomachs, and when they burn down to charred, fiberglass filter, we flick them into trash cans and potted plants. We laugh when we miss.

The Antique Mall is in Meridian Plaza, an ill-planned shopping center on the west side of town. A girl in our apartment building is dating the senior who works there, and she told us that the cameras in every corner are just for show. She knows because she fucked him on the antique iron bed on the second floor.

The store is divided into a dozen rooms between the two floors, and each room has up to four booths where the elderly, overconfident in their collections, ply rusted salt and pepper shakers for forty dollars. Most of the booths keep their jewelry locked behind plexiglass cases, but booth number twenty-four, in the furthest corner of the second floor, is careless. A mahogany desk (tagged at $675) holds felt-lined boxes filled with gawdy, gold-link chains and the occasional gemstone. An oversized ring catches our eye, a wide, silver high school class ring with a bright blue stone: Class of 1973. We empty them one by one into our purses, not bothering to untangle the chains.

On our way out, we spot a gold Zippo lighter next to the register. Another shopper has called the pimply senior to her assistance ("$700?" she squawks), and we understand that the Zippo is ours and has been waiting for us. We pocket it.

The first Zippo came off the line in 1933, with its brass casing, spring-flip lid, and flint wheel ignition. It was a popular product, and it became especially popular in the military. During World War II, the company closed commercial production and manufactured Zippos for the American military. With the wartime shortage of brass, they opted to use steel instead. After the war, the lighters became a working-class status symbol and a valuable collector's item. A Zippo was a man's lighter, and a man used a Zippo.

We are seventeen, and I am holding your hair back while you vomit into an empty doorway. We are drunk, and it frightens me. The party is blocks behind, but we are not yet far enough away from the cacophonous howls of teenagers in the throes of Bacardi Gold. You heave one last time, and I pick you up, and we walk again, staggering against each other. The stadium lights of the Walmart parking lot are just ahead, and we lurch toward them like moths to a bug zapper. We will go there and become ourselves again.

The Walmart is bright and white, rows and rows of product nearly glowing in the fluorescence. The cold, medicinal air of the store hits us in waves and calms the rum in our blood.

We are home among the aisles of board games, Barbie dolls, children's bicycles, party supplies, greeting cards, Harlequin romance novels, Mr. Coffees, economy-sized Rubbermaid tubs, and flimsy fast-fashion clothing.

"Let's play a game," you say. You steady yourself against a metal cage filled with rubber balls. "Whoever gets the most wins."

You take off into Home Decor and I curse my choice to bring a clutch purse to the party. It occurs to me that you didn't bring a purse at all, and this makes me feel a little better. I cruise down the party supply aisle and stuff a light-up suction ball, a bag of small infant-shaped party favors, and a packet of Happy Birthday napkins into the clutch. Then three packages of amphibian stickers and a box of American Flag toothpicks. My purse is bulging, and I hear the creaking of a stock cart inching along somewhere nearby. I zip my purse and hook a left into the pharmacy section. The black-globe eye of the store's cameras burns into my scalp. I am drunk, it occurs to me, and I am still afraid.

I hurry to Home Decor and comb the aisles for you. Panic begins to fill my stomach and I know I'm going to vomit, but first I have to find you.

"Miss?" I whirl around, and it isn't you—of course, it's not—but a middle-aged woman with a meth-lined face and the store's blue, happy face emblazoned vest.

I nearly choke as saliva fills my mouth. I nod. She offers me a four-pack set of Martha Stewart Living Tea Towels.

"I found them in beige like you were looking for," she says. She smiles, and her teeth look like the pier at the lake after a dry summer. "Is there anything else I can help you with?"

The walkie-talkie on her belt crackles. "No, thank you," I manage.

I take the towels and walk away as fast as I can, trying to make my urgent departure look casual, but I feel my heel wobble with each step. I glance over my shoulder and the woman is already gone, but I hear you, I hear you giggling. And suddenly there you are, in an outfit I've never seen, laughing at me.

"I'm going to be sick," I say.

You wave your hand at me, two shiny new rings on your index and middle finger. "Oh, calm down. She wasn't gonna do anything. Did you see those teeth?"

"No, I'm going to be sick," I say, and then I have to run because I feel the acidity in my teeth and I know I can't stop it.

I make it outside in time to puke on the median that divides the parking lot. It is late enough that there aren't many cars in the lot and there is no one to see me curled over in the grass. I wait for you to tuck my hair behind my ears, but you don't, so I do it myself. I spit the last of my sickness into the grass and stand.

"Sorry," I say, wiping my mouth on the back of my sleeve.

But you're not there. I see you across the street next to the car wash, your arms crossed. "Let's go!" you shout, though the sound carries dimly. I stare for a moment, and you stamp your feet like we did when we were little. You are my mirror, but I cannot recognize your face. Is that lipstick?

I go to you, and we do not speak as we walk home. On the way I toss my clutch into a dumpster, filled with its knickknacks and cheap crap. You win the game and a thick, alkali taste bites at the back of my throat. You do not ask if I'm okay, and I don't tell you.

HOLD TIGHT

The white bread smushed softly against Deirdre's chest as she tried to balance the jar of mayonnaise, the pimento loaf, and the package of sixteen American cheese singles. She added up the total—seven dollars plus tax—pulling a crumpled wad of bills from her front pocket; she tried to smooth them out on her thigh. Yes, it would be enough, with a little leftover.

It was Sunday, and the morning services had just let out, the parishioners flocking to the supermarket for honey hams and boxes of dehydrated scalloped potatoes. This was the set she tried to avoid. Her skin burned as their eyes scanned over her, registering her messy hair, cut-off jean shorts, an oversized tank top. She stuck out in the midst of the below-the-knee skirts and tasteful collars.

An older woman pushed past her to reach the pickles, nudging her arm with an oversized lavender handbag. The mayonnaise tipped.

The shattering of glass almost overpowered the sugary music that pumped out of the store's speakers. She felt the sharp bite of the shards, then the cool wet of the mayonnaise as it splashed across her bare calves. The older woman shrieked. Her silk shoes were drenched.

"You should be more careful," the woman said. She clutched her bag close as if Deirdre might snatch it.

Deirdre wrapped her arms tightly around her groceries. Her throat tightened, and she couldn't bring herself to speak. Her head down, she rushed to the register and dumped the items on the conveyor belt. She vaguely registered the blood trickling onto her flip-flop. The woman was still screaming in aisle five.

"You alright? Sounded like a mess back there," the young cashier said brightly.

Deirdre nodded. "Someone dropped something, is all." She barely recognized her voice.

Her baby was a boy, Josie, born in Lusa, in the little twelve-bed IHS hospital that served the southern half of the county. Deirdre was married then, and young—too young, she realized now. Her husband, Danny, worked at the gristmill, just a few blocks away. The job paid decent even if it was only five months out of the year. Money was tight in the off-season, but the bosses quietly encouraged the workers to draw unemployment during the rest of the year, which helped.

They lived happily enough in a single-wide trailer with green plastic siding across the street from Lusa's only park. For a town whose Main Street boasted two burned-out storefronts among a cluster of secondhand shops and a hardware store, waking up to the park each morning was a prized view, and Deirdre was especially proud of the flower boxes she'd set up along their white plastic fence. Theirs was the prettiest yard on the block. Every morning, she'd make Danny breakfast and take Josie outside, propping him up in a baby bouncer as she received a steady stream of morning admirers. She knew some of the neighborhood women lusted after Danny, with his strong, tanned shoulders and easy laugh, but that only made her prouder that she was his wife and she had the baby to prove it.

She could hear the kids screaming as soon as she got out of the store. "Quiet down, guys," she said, her voice thin. The Impala's trunk didn't shut quite right, so after she threw the groceries in the back, she kneeled to clip the bungee cord that held the trunk to the car's bumper. Josie leaned too far out of the back window.

"Sit down," she said.

Josie sunk into the backseat. The horn beeped, a strangled whistle, and from the corner of her eye, Deirdre saw the littler ones, Tate and Paige, scrambling over the front bench seat, giggling. With a hard tug, she clipped the bungee cord and slapped the side panel as she pushed herself up.

"I saw that."

Tate dropped into the small gap between front and back seats, but Paige was slower, and Deirdre swatted her leg through the open window. The little girl began to cry.

"I can't leave you alone for ten minutes," Deirdre said. She fell into the driver's seat and slammed her door. "Josie, get in the front." The boy pressed himself against the back seat. "Now. You two, buckle up."

Once the kids settled, she started the engine and backed out of the lot. It groaned and shook. She pumped the gas pedal to even out the rattling.

"Do you think you can behave for one day? Just one?" she said.

"I wanna go back to Grandma's," Paige whispered.

"Well, you can't, okay?" Deirdre said. Her throat bubbled; she refused to cry. "You heard what she said. We're out."

"She said *you're* out," Tate said quietly. Deirdre watched him play with his shoelaces in the backseat.

"So where are we going then?" Josie asked. He held his hands in his lap like a good boy.

"Do you remember that park we used to live by in Lusa? The one with the big tree and the merry-go-round you liked?"

Paige sniffled in the backseat, but she wasn't crying anymore. Deirdre sneaked a look at her youngest in the rearview mirror: She'd grown in the last couple of months, and she badly needed a haircut. Paige's moppy, brown hair was dirty enough that it had started to mat itself into tight strings.

"Isn't that kinda far, Mom?" he asked. Such a good boy, Josie, and smart. Deirdre smiled at him.

"I've got it all taken care of, hon," she said. "You wanna pick the radio station?"

She took a left on Main and headed toward the highway. Josie clicked on the radio and started skimming through the stations. Paul Harvey's gravelly bass rattled out between the waves of static.

The grassy plains gave way to warbling hills and tightly knit clusters of trees. There weren't many cars on the road that afternoon. A few semitrucks sped ahead of the Impala, riding close as they caught each other's tailwinds. Tate squealed as a band of bikers on Harleys rumbled down the old highway. They dipped in and out of view with every hill.

The old highway was built on a trail broken in by the local tribes, but most everyone took the more direct interstate. If she had more gas, she'd have taken the old way. Deirdre hadn't even been born when the interstate was built, but the old highway held a handful of her teenage haunts. The two-lane blacktop snaked alongside the river, sometimes turning in on itself. Behind one of the curves, well out of sight of the interstate, was the spillway. During the summer months, the water filled a red rock basin and flooded the creek banks before emptying into the reservoir.

Her mother had picked her up there a few times, after she missed curfew or when the sheriffs showed up. It was only ever beers, maybe a bottle of liquor, but her mother acted as if a half dozen teenagers getting drunk in the woods was the pinnacle of vice. Everything was dire with her mother. Whenever she'd call, hysterical over this or that, Danny would just laugh and shake his head. He'd handled her so much better than Deirdre ever had. If he'd been there this morning, Deirdre was sure that she'd still be in her mother's kitchen, the kids playing in the backyard.

"Josie, hon, can you light Mama a smoke?" she asked; her hands shook, and she tightened her grip on the steering wheel. "They're in my purse."

"Grandma said you quit smoking," he said.

"Well, I didn't," she said. She pushed her bag toward him with her elbow. "Inside zipper. Can't miss 'em."

He dug around her purse for a second before he found them, a crushed soft pack of menthol 100's and a pink Bic. A pang of guilt shot through Deirdre, and she sucked in her breath; her son held a cigarette like a pencil as he waved the flame below the tip.

"It stinks," Paige whined.

"The windows are down, baby," Deirdre said, the cigarette hanging loosely from her lips. "I don't know what else you want me to do."

Paige twisted her hair into knots. "Are we there yet?"

"Shut up," Tate told her. "You're annoying."

Josie turned in his seat and popped Tate on his bare knee. The younger boy yipped like a puppy.

"Quit it, guys," Deirdre said through gritted teeth.

"He hit me," Tate said. "It's his fault!"

"Is not."

"Is too."

"Guys—" They talked over her, their voices shrill enough she wanted to cover her ears. "C'mon, guys—"

Deirdre slammed on the brakes and wrenched the car to the shoulder. The tires growled against the rumble strips. She flicked her spent cigarette out the window and, unbuckling her seat belt, got out of the car. Tate and Paige were quiet now, trying to make themselves small. Deirdre covered her face with her hands. The gust from a passing semi pushed her against the car.

"Mom?" Josie called. "Mama?"

The passenger door clicked open, and Deirdre slapped the top of the car.

"Don't," she said.

Deirdre got back in the car, letting out a heavy sigh as she sank into the driver's seat. She gripped the steering wheel at ten and two.

"Mommy?" It was Paige.

"Okay," Deirdre breathed. "Okay. There's a picnic in the trunk. Can you hold tight for just a little longer? Can you do that for me?"

Her children nodded. The car lurched back onto the highway.

When Josie was three, Danny started to talk about cutting the toddler's hair. He was born with a thick shock of black hair, and Deirdre insisted on letting it grow. It was nearly to the middle of his back, glossy and thick with a slight curl at the ends, though it had lightened quite a bit by then. Josie was tall for his age, and his face had already thinned to that of a little boy, but his hair was as soft as a newborn's. She loved to pull his hair into two little braids and wrap them with cotton ribbons. Danny worried that Josie'd be bullied, that he'd be called a sissy. But he wasn't a sissy, Deirdre insisted, he was a warrior.

In the eighth month of her pregnancy with Tate, her blood pressure skyrocketed, and a regular checkup became an hour-long ambulance ride. The harvest had finished, so Danny and Josie were there with her, though there wasn't enough room in the ambulance for them.

The city hospital was so different from the one in Lusa. There were elevators, wards, locked doors, and dozens of nurses and doctors running back and forth in blue scrubs and long, white lab coats. So many people, and yet she was alone in a bright, white room that smelled of antiseptic. The operation had been quick: A few sticks in her spine for the epidural, and then the agonizing feeling of a doctor tugging at her organs, pulling them back to get at the baby inside her. Though she was numb, she felt acutely disconnected from her body at the feel of a nurse's fingertips holding her uterus open just inches from her face.

It was hours before the nurses wheeled Tate into her room. He was so small, the little blue cap much too big for him, hanging loose around his ears. The nurses gave her a bottle of formula and warned her against breastfeeding until the pain medications wore off. They left her alone to feed him, and once they'd gone she gently tugged the cap off. Beneath it, he was bald, and the fluorescent hospital lights shadowed the thumbprint of his soft spot. His skin was like paper, like a little, paper doll. She held him close. His eyes were the color of the reservoir at night, almost purple.

Danny and Josie were late. Danny promised, as she'd been wheeled into the ambulance, that he would be there, but hours passed and he didn't come. She cried, and Tate cried, and then the nurses took him away again to put him under the jaundice light.

Later, when she woke from the morphine sleep, they were there, her husband and her sons. Danny sat in the rigid bedside chair with Josie in his lap, the two of them holding a swaddled Tate in their arms. She smiled groggily at them, and they smiled back. As her vision cleared and her family took shape, she saw what was missing: Josie's hair was parted down the middle, hanging loose at his chin. His braids were gone.

Once they were back on the road, Tate and Paige slumped against the doors and slept. It was hot, and beads of sweat collected on their softened faces. Paige's hair stuck to her neck. It was sweltering out, but the windows were only open a crack in an effort to keep out the dirt and dust that clouded the air, tossed in thick plumes from the backs of combines that zigged and zagged through the fields that ran alongside the highway. Josie didn't speak as he flipped back and forth between a country and an oldies station.

Deirdre used to think the fields were beautiful, the way the winter wheat grew in such perfect, manicured rows, dense and inscrutable in its pattern except for at that perfect angle when its order revealed itself. And then the combines, carving out crop circles in the fields. There was beauty in it, even if Danny was called away for almost days at a time to handle the night deliveries to the gristmill.

Not many men wanted the overnight shifts, and the mill weighed their shorthandedness against the sheer volume of work to be done. Deirdre knew it was hard work, and she was grateful. Some nights Danny would be the overseer, others he'd be working the chutes that poured the grain into huge silos. Others still, he'd be inside the silo, working the grain when it stuck to the sides or gummed up the end of a chute. On nights he worked the silos, he'd come home wearing a layer of fine dust, so much that his dark eyelashes were white with it, and she'd make him take off his coveralls outside. Sometimes Deirdre wondered if that was cruel of her.

"Want one?" Josie asked.

His voice surprised her, and she gasped. He raised her cigarettes and lighter. She shook her head slowly. Josie was only ten; he shouldn't be playing with a lighter. She touched his hair, tucked it behind his ear. She squeezed his knee.

"No, thanks, baby," she whispered. "Our exit's just up here."

"Mom," Josie began, "where are we really going?"

"To the park," she said, "I already told you."

"No, but after," he replied. "Grandma said—"

"Grandma says a lot of things."

"Yeah, but—"

"But nothing."

Paige startled awake in the back, and Josie glanced at his sister, then Deirdre. He shushed Paige and pressed his finger to his lips. He was so grown-up. With every season he was more and more his father's son. Deirdre fumbled for her cigarettes without looking and, her hands shaking, lit one. The nicotine calmed her nerves as she held the steering wheel with one hand. She flipped the turn signal and guided the Impala onto the off-ramp.

Tate was just a few months old when she found out she was pregnant again. With every passing day, the hard knot grew until she couldn't lift Tate without feeling a tiny, itching tear inside her. Lifting Josie was out of the question. There were mornings when the nausea was so bad that she prayed it would end, that this baby would just slip out of her without a breath. This baby took too much, wanted too much.

Danny knew. He saw it in the way her face fell with the boys' every cry and whimper. He took them out of the house before she woke, to the park or to friends' houses, and they'd return late in the evening toting bags of fast food for her to sniff at. While they were gone, Deirdre's mother would visit. She said she was there to help, but all she did was make Deirdre out to be a bad mother, an irresponsible mother. Another baby in such a small house, another baby with two babies already. Deirdre had been so stupid: The doctor was right there when Tate was born. She should've had her tubes tied then and there. And Danny's salary barely supported a family of three, much less a family of five. And the bills from having Tate, in a private hospital no less—stupid, reckless Deirdre.

She couldn't tell Danny what her mother said while he was out with their sons. His mother died when he was young, and he took hers as his own, even though her mother never had anything good to say about him. She thought he was lazy. She thought he didn't work hard enough to move them into a real house, to find a job with benefits. Maybe he didn't.

In late June, Danny went back to work, and her mother began to stay over when he pulled a graveyard shift. The night it happened, her mother shook her awake to the chaos of flashing lights and sirens. Half asleep, Deirdre was suspicious of her mother as she tugged on her ratty bathrobe and followed her to the porch.

"Something's going on over there," her mother said excitedly. "What do you think it is?"

"I'm gonna check on the boys, Ma," Deirdre said sleepily. "I'm sure it's fine."

"No, look!" her mother demanded, pinching her elbow. "They're all over at the mill. Lord, I didn't even know Lusa had that many cops."

Deirdre shook her mother off and started down the porch steps and into the street. The asphalt was cold against her bare feet but she kept going, clutching the neck of her bathrobe. She walked through the park and made to round the corner.

Her mother called after her, but she didn't pause. As she got closer to the mill, she had to shield her eyes as police, fire, and ambulance lights strobed and reflected off the shiny steel silos. The county sheriff and the tribal police were there, and another fire truck from two towns over. She made it to the fire truck before anyone stopped her, a heavyset sheriff with a trimmed mustache.

"Ma'am, you can't go in there," he said. She tried to push past him, and he gripped her shoulders.

"My husband," Deirdre whispered, "my husband works here." She saw Tim, another millworker, crouched against the side of a police car, a brown blanket wrapped tight around his shoulders. "Tim."

Tim's head lolled around before he saw and then his face fell. The lights illuminated his wet face, and he buried his head between his knees. He wouldn't look at her. Deirdre felt herself falling, but it didn't occur that she should catch herself until the sheriff picked her up around her middle and hoisted her into the passenger seat of an empty car.

"Ma'am?" he asked. "Ma'am? Are you Mrs. Daniel Teller?"

She nodded. His lips moved, and she noted how his mustache twitched as he spoke. He was telling her something, but she heard as if from underwater, the thick roar of blood in her ears muting him. Then her mother was there, speaking with the sheriff, and Deirdre was being led home. Her foot was bleeding. Her mother smoothed her hair and kissed her forehead as they walked.

"He couldn't get out," her mother was saying. "No air in there."

"No air?"

The park was in full late summer bloom, and the sun shone green through the thick elm trees. She pulled the car up in front of their old place, but the lot was empty and overgrown. A section of the fence was still up, but it was cracked and brown. The mailbox had been bashed in and hung limply off the broken fence.

"We're here," Deirdre sang. "Wake up, wake up, we're here!"

Tate and Paige stirred and got out of the car, rubbing sleep from their eyes, as Deirdre got the food out of the trunk. Paige ran to a spigot just inside the park. She lifted the pump and drank from it, with Tate not far behind her. Josie kicked at the grass.

"Don't drink too much, y'all," Deirdre warned. "Jo, honey? Let's go find a table."

She picked a table underneath the largest tree in the park. The table had been painted red in the last decade, but now it was the same rusty color as the iron-rich dirt that spread around the base of the tree. She emptied the shopping bag onto the table and lined up the bread, the pimento loaf, and the cheese, side by side. Josie sat across from her.

"Where's our house?" he asked.

"I don't know," she said. "Landlord might've moved it, maybe sold it. I don't know."

She took six slices from behind the bread's heel and laid them out on the table. She peeled open the pimento loaf and laid a piece on each slice, then unwrapped three American singles and laid them over the meat. Josie propped his elbows up and put his head down.

"Not hungry?" Deirdre asked him.

She whistled, and Paige and Tate came running, the fronts of their shirts dripping. They scrambled onto the bench and snatched their sandwiches. Paige hungrily stuffed hers into her mouth while Tate carefully removed the crusts of his.

"Is dry," Paige mumbled around her sandwich.

"You're welcome," Deirdre replied. "Now eat up, and you can go play."

The park had changed in five years. The maypole swing was gone, and in its place was a brightly colored plastic jungle gym. In the park's center, there had been a small pond, stocked with cast-off Easter ducks and a few fat goldfish, but it looked to have been filled in with white sand, and the hedges that halved the park were gone. The hedges had been a bit of a nuisance, blocking the view from one side of the park to the other. The merry-go-round was still there, though, and a few kids, none of whom Deirdre recognized, held onto the platform's crisscrossed bars as a bigger boy threw his weight behind every push.

"Finish!" Paige clapped her hands together and opened her mouth wide, sticking out her tongue.

"Me, too," Tate said.

Tate rolled his bread crusts into balls and lined them up. He was such a tidy child, always picking up after himself and his sister. While Paige was like a spinning top, he was calm, even-tempered. Those years in her mother's house, he'd always been eager to please. Her mother taught him to bake, a skill Deirdre never had the patience for. Deirdre stroked the boy's hand.

"Well, what are you waiting for? Go on," she said.

Paige sprinted to the tallest slide, Tate a few steps behind. Josie pushed his sandwich toward her.

"I'm not hungry, Mom," he said. "You eat it."

"If you don't like the pickles in it, you can just pick 'em out," Deirdre said, "I thought you liked—"

"Mom," Josie interrupted. "What's gonna happen to us?"

"I can't tell the future." Deirdre lit a cigarette and flicked the first ash onto the bench.

"That's not what I mean," he said.

Across the park, Paige scrambled into a baby swing and called for Tate to push her. Deirdre waved at them, but they didn't see her.

"If you're not gonna eat, go make sure they stay out of trouble," she said.

Josie stared at her before standing. He picked up his sandwich and, as he walked over to the swings, tossed it in the blue trash can. Deirdre sighed. He'd be eleven soon, and she worried about him. He carried too much for a boy his age.

Deirdre exhaled, and the menthol cooled her throat. Menthol had been Danny's flavor of choice, a habit she picked up after the accident. Patches, pills, none of it felt as good as rolling the filter between her fingers as it burned. None of it smelled like that thick, sweet smell that lingered in her clothes and in her hair.

Her children were on the merry-go-round now. Josie pushed while Tate tucked his legs underneath him as he gripped the bars. Paige sprawled belly down in the center, squealing with every turn. Her daughter hadn't gotten a fair shake, Deirdre knew that now. She couldn't take care of her babies, and when Paige was born, Deirdre couldn't hold her for more than a few minutes at a time. Just the baby girl's smell made her stomach seize up.

They had each other; so long as they had each other, they'd be okay.

Deirdre began walking to the other end of the park. She crossed the street, walking faster now. The houses here hadn't changed. If anything, the mock Sears houses looked nicer than they did before, like something from the cover of *Southern Living*. The mill's closing didn't hurt these families any. She rounded the corner and began to run. Chains blocked the old entrance, but she easily ducked between them and kept going. The air was quiet, save for the locusts' hum.

The silos were still there, beneath years of dirt and rust, still the tallest things Lusa had to offer. She rested her palms against the base of the center silo. He'd been in this one, like he had so many other times. That summer was unusually wet, and the grain gummed up inside, blocking the silo's auger. He was strong and he knew not to let go of the safety ladder that led down into the grain bin. But he did, he let go, and when the ground gave way beneath him, he went under. When she identified the body, the sheriff told her it had been quick, that he hadn't suffered. The weight of the grain crushed him in just seconds. His handsome face was bruised but wasn't swollen.

She pressed her cheek to the side of the bin, and it warmed her. It wasn't anyone's fault. Not Paige's, the boys', Danny's, or hers. It was an accident.

In the distance, she heard them calling for her, yelling first then screaming. She sat back against the silo and pulled her knees up. She laid her head in her hands and began to cry.

Acknowledgments

I want to thank my editor and mentor, Lily Hoang, and Elizabeth Earley and Vanessa Daunais for believing in this project. I'd also like to thank Anjali Singh and Evan Lavender-Smith for providing much-needed encouragement and insight along the way. Rus Bradburd, without whose confidence in me I'd have never met Lily, thank you. Anjali Singh and Sunday Coward, thank you so much for your professional and personal guidance—without you, I wouldn't be where or who I am today. To my dearest friend Gen DesGeorges, you make me believe I can do anything. And an especially heartfelt thank you to my husband, Ross Howerton: Thank you for believing in me and never giving up on me.

CPSIA information can be obtained
at www.ICGtesting.com
Printed in the USA
LVHW040211300123
738200LV00005B/342